CHANGE ME UP

Vivienne's Vacation
Tempting Tenealle

Berengaria Brown

MENAGE AND MORE

Siren Publishing, Inc.
www.SirenPublishing.com

A SIREN PUBLISHING BOOK
IMPRINT: Ménage and More

CHANGE ME UP
Vivienne's Vacation
Tempting Tenealle
Copyright © 2011 by Berengaria Brown

ISBN-10: 1-61034-921-0
ISBN-13: 978-1-61034-921-5

First Printing: August 2011

Cover design by Jinger Heaston
All cover art and logo copyright © 2011 by Siren Publishing, Inc.

ALL RIGHTS RESERVED: This literary work may not be reproduced or transmitted in any form or by any means, including electronic or photographic reproduction, in whole or in part, without express written permission.

All characters and events in this book are fictitious. Any resemblance to actual persons living or dead is strictly coincidental.

Printed in the U.S.A.

PUBLISHER
Siren Publishing, Inc.
www.SirenPublishing.com

DEDICATIONS

Vivienne's Vacation

To erotic romance author Elizabeth Lapthorne who introduced me to e-books.

Tempting Tenealle

For my bazillion cousins: the fun ones, the helpful ones, the caring ones, and the plain weird ones. I love you all.

Siren Publishing
Ménage & More

Vivienne's Vacation

BERENGARIA BROWN

VIVIENNE'S VACATION

BERENGARIA BROWN
Copyright © 2011

PART I

Chapter One

Vivienne was ready.

She was wearing her brand-new, oh-so-tiny purple silk bra and panties. Her nails, both fingers and toes, had been painted a matching purple. The beautician had also shampooed her long brown hair and touched up the little signs of gray at the roots, then exfoliated her everywhere—absolutely everywhere—before massaging lavender oil into her skin.

Vivi hadn't known whether to blush or giggle, but now, she certainly looked and felt mighty good for someone who had turned forty last year.

And now the time had come. Well, almost.

She looked at the clock on the entertainment center again. One minute to go.

Butterflies swirled in her stomach, and for a moment, she considered calling it all off.

"Adam and Ben, Superior Vacations, ma'am," came a deep male voice simultaneously with a knock on the door.

I can't do this! But dammit, I want to do it, and I will.

Vivi looked through the peephole. One tall, dark hunk, and one slightly shorter, blond hunk, both wearing Superior Vacations polo shirts.

Exactly what she had ordered.

She opened the door and stood to the side.

The blond entered first, a laptop bag over his shoulder with "Superior Vacations" engraved on the flap. "Adam," he said.

"And Ben," added the dark-haired one.

As she drew in a deep breath to control the butterflies, she caught the slight scent of something spicy, and surprisingly, her panties dampened.

Adam placed the laptop bag on the entertainment center and spoke in that deep voice that sent shivers right to her cunt. "You look absolutely delicious in that outfit. Let us give you an evening you will never forget."

Ben moved closer and very slowly drew her into his arms. "You're one hot chick, Vivienne. Or would you like to be called Vivi?" His arms tightened around her, and he pressed his body against hers.

"Vivi," she whispered.

His chest was a solid wall of muscle under the black Superior Vacations polo shirt. And his black jeans did nothing to disguise a cock that was a hard ridge against her belly. She shivered slightly as his hands smoothed up and down her back, and he bent his head to kiss gently at her chin, her ear, and then her mouth.

She opened to his urging, and his tongue thrust inside her mouth, running around the insides of her cheeks, the back of her teeth, then tangling with her tongue.

Ben sucked her tongue into his mouth as he increased the pressure on her lips, and she melted into his sensuous kiss.

God, he can kiss!

Hands began to run up and down her legs, smoothing around her ankles, then one foot was lifted up, and a toe was sucked into a warm, sexy mouth.

My God! Cream released from her cunt onto her panties while her belly clenched and need clawed at her pussy.

Vivienne's Vacation

Ben's lips roved along her neck, her shoulder, her earlobe, while Adam's moved up to suck behind her knee. A knee that was wobbling from the sensations running through her.

Without saying a word, the men lifted her and carried her to the bed, laying her flat, and fingers removed her lingerie while mouths continued to drive her need higher and higher with kisses all over her body.

"I do love a bare cunt," whispered Adam as he began kissing and licking her slit.

"And these breasts are lush, ripe, and just begging to be sucked," added Ben, suiting actions to words as he drew one into his talented mouth.

Hands were touching, smoothing, caressing her thighs, her belly, her breasts. Need coiled inside her, rising higher, higher.

"I want..."

But before she could say anything further, a tongue thrust into her mouth, and fingers plunged into her cunt. Three fingers that curled upward and scraped her sweet spot just as another hand pinched her nipple.

Tension exploded in Vivi, and she came, shaking and gasping.

The fingers in her cunt soothed and gentled her as she rode the waves of the orgasm while feather-soft kisses whispered across her eyelids, nose, and mouth.

When Vivi opened her eyes, Adam was naked in front of her, rolling a condom on his engorged cock. Ben climbed off the bed and began undressing as Adam started kissing her cunt again. Within moments, Vivienne's nerve endings were on fire once more.

"Fuck me now," she gasped hoarsely, and Adam pulled her thighs wider apart and slid inside her.

With long, slow thrusts, he angled his cock so that every stroke pressed on her G-spot. He grabbed her legs, pushing her thighs as wide as they would go and pressing her feet flat on the bed, shifting his body to maintain a steady pace that had her panting and whimpering, wanting more. More.

Ben appeared by her head, his cock dark red with need. Uncircumcised as she had requested. Placing it close to her lips, he said, "Go on. Suck it. Run your tongue under the foreskin. Feel the difference. Taste it."

She reached up a hand and softly touched his cock, then held the root and sucked in the head, rolling the foreskin down with her tongue and laving the head then pushing the protective skin back over it again.

Ben gasped and said, "That's it, Vivi. Jeez, that's wonderful. Keep doing that."

Adam let go of her thighs, holding her steady with a hand on her hip, and stroked her breast with his other hand. Ben's hand joined in on the other side, and Vivi lost the power of thought. All she could do was feel. Feel the hands massaging her breasts, nails running over her nipples and areolas, fingers tweaking her hard points. The cock pounding into her cunt, dragging along her sensitive walls, hitting her sweet spot on every thrust.

The cock in her mouth, filling it, soft skin over hard muscle, and the taste of salty drops of cum.

Ben began to thrust into her mouth, synchronizing each plunge with Adam's cock in her pussy. The hands on her breasts moved faster, harder. Need rose in Vivi, demanding more, harder, something—but her mouth was too full to talk, her brain too scrambled by need to form words.

A finger began circling her anus, round and round, making the nerves there skitter with need.

"Suck me!" yelled Ben.

Vivi drew in her cheeks hard and sucked with all her strength.

Adam slammed deeply into her cunt, fingers pinched her nipples hard, and another finger pushed deep into her anus.

Vivi exploded in crashing waves of orgasm, her cunt squeezing Adam's cock like a vise, causing him to come, too, and they both brought Ben along with them, his cum splashing hot against the back of her throat.

The men gentled their movements, soothing, patting, caressing, kissing Vivi softly, and smoothing her strained muscles as the aftershocks from her orgasm rolled through her.

"Thank you," she whispered, sinking back onto the mattress as they arranged her limbs in a more comfortable position and pulled the coverlet over her. Adam moved off her, rolling her onto her side and pulling her against him. Ben moved in behind her, snuggling close, with his arm stretched over her.

Warm, satiated, exhausted, Vivi slept.

* * * *

An hour later, Vivi woke to two mouths sucking her toes. Shivers ran up and down her body, and her cunt clenched.

The mouths moved up her legs, sucking behind her knees, kissing up her thighs, then tongues licked the crease between leg and torso.

"Oh my God. That is unbelievable. What a way to wake up."

"That is just the start," said Adam. "We have much more planned for you."

"Starting right here," added Ben, kissing her bare mons and sucking her clit into his mouth.

"And here." Adam's mouth reached a breast, sucking the nipple in and rolling it around with his tongue.

"God," she whimpered, as her cunt started to drip honey and desire rolled through her body.

Adam lifted Vivi and slid underneath her body, his mouth sucking the sensitive point where her neck and shoulder joined. His hands reached around and grasped her nipples, rolling and squeezing them to bullet-hard points.

Ben was already wearing a condom, she noticed, as he slipped between her thighs and thrust in one long, hard push inside her cunt.

He rubbed his chest hard against Adam's hands, making the friction on her nipples an exquisite pleasure-pain, and drove his tongue forcefully into her mouth, matching his thrusts with his cock.

Adam's hands moved from her breasts, one sliding between her body and Ben's to brush Ben's cock and her clit, sending hot shivers through both of them.

The other hand slid between her body and his, fingering her anus and his own cock.

The men developed a coordinated thrust, cocks, tongues, and hands all moving together, and Vivi began to pant with need. They increased the pace until her whole body was one big nerve ending demanding more.

Inside her cunt, excitement curled harder and tighter. The friction was exquisite and demanding, but she needed more. More.

Ben lifted up a little from her body, angling his cock to slam against her G-spot with every thrust. Adam's cock rested between the cheeks of her ass, rubbing up and down on her skin. His hands moved to her breasts again and pinched her nipples as his teeth sank into the muscle of her neck.

She strained for release, digging her nails into Ben's shoulders as his fingers came down and pinched her clit.

"Yes! Yes! Yes!" Vivi screamed, shattering into a million pieces.

Ben's other hand slid over the taut cheeks of Adam's ass, a finger pushed into his anus, and the two men climaxed together. The hot seed splashing against her butt cheeks and the throbbing and pulsing cock in her cunt kept Vivi's orgasm rolling through her.

After a few more thrusts, the guys pressed soft, light kisses to Vivi's face and back as they withdrew.

"Sleep now," whispered Ben, rolling her onto her side.

"Dream of us," added Adam, pulling the coverlet over her.

My toes really did curl when I came. I thought that was just a myth. Then Vivi fell asleep.

* * * *

It was midmorning before Vivienne woke and dragged herself into the bathroom. She started the taps running to fill the huge hot tub then stumbled back into the other room to make herself some coffee.

Half an hour later, she was warm and relaxed, the kinks uncurling from her overused muscles, lying back sipping her second cup of coffee in the tub while the jets massaged her back.

As a youth social worker, Vivienne had helped many homeless teenage girls to gain life skills and job skills. But part of listening to them and mentoring them involved hearing their stories. And although not one of the girls she worked with was legally old enough to have sex, their experience astounded her. In fact, it was harder and harder for her to offer relevant advice as she could scarcely even imagine some of the situations these young girls put themselves in.

I'm turning into a staid old prude. Just because I'm divorced doesn't mean I can't have sex anymore.

But I don't want a one-night stand with a guy I meet at a party or something like these kids do.

I want safety, boundaries, to experience what I've missed out on—not boring, average sex.

A week of evenings spent trolling the internet gave Vivi a list of things she wanted to do and the names of several companies who provided such services—for a fee.

So here she was in a four-star hotel in a different state on a two-week vacation. She had four specific sexual experiences planned with a day off between each to recover and an intimate piercing booked on day nine, leaving her with a few days to heal from it before going home.

"And yum, the first taste of two men was very, very successful," she said, toasting Adam and Ben with her coffee cup. "Those guys were truly delicious. Hunky but caring. And very, very good at their job. And my first real-life look at and taste of an uncircumcised cock was interesting, too."

Vivi shivered and sank down deeper in the tub with the thought of tomorrow.

Two men simultaneously. Anal and vaginal. Caleb and David.

"Adam, Ben, Caleb, David. Then Eli, Frank, and George. Strictly alphabetical, so I can't forget who's next. I wonder if they have trouble remembering who they are." She laughed.

Well, Adam and Ben had been worth every cent of their fee.

Vivi's marriage had been fine, nothing outstanding but good enough. She and her college boyfriend had married right after graduation. The sex had been okay, not earth-shattering, but mostly she'd gotten orgasms out of it. Then they had both concentrated on their careers. And one day, they'd realized they had nothing in common anymore, nothing even to talk about.

After the divorce, Vivi had continued to focus on her career, loving her work with teens, teaching them to cook and to budget, to drive a car, helping improve their literacy and numeracy skills, and providing them with techniques on how to succeed in an interview for a job.

She'd even had a couple of boyfriends, but her hours were crazy, and it seemed like she always had to be in hospital or in court with one of the girls whenever a big date night was scheduled.

This system was much better. This way she got hot sex guaranteed with the experiences she wanted and no danger.

* * * *

The secretary handed over a thick booklet.

Vivienne's Vacation *15*

"Be sure you answer every question, ma'am. Your partners will be chosen to fulfill your requirements, so it is very important you check the boxes for exactly what you want."

Q2 Hair color: blond or dark?
Oh, one of each, definitely, she thought.
…
Q24 Cock: long or thick?
Oh, wow, perhaps I could have one of each of those, too. Then I could answer that age-old question as to which is better.
…
Q75 Piercings: nose, eyebrow, tongue, nipple, cock?
A tongue stud would be interesting. I'd like to kiss a man with a tongue stud. And a nipple ring, I might even consider having one of those myself. I'll definitely think about that. A pierced cock—do I dare to fuck a man with a pierced cock?

"Ma'am? Ma'am? Are you finished? It's time for your interview now."

"What? Yes, thank you."

Vivi shook off the memories and climbed out of the tub, focusing on some sightseeing for the rest of the day. And a meal. It was nearly noon, and she was starving after all that exercise last night.

Chapter Two

After a lunch of squid in black bean sauce made with Chinese salted black beans in a Cantonese restaurant, Vivienne spent the afternoon wandering around Chinatown enjoying the sights and sounds. She pottered in and out of dozens of tiny, crammed stores and purchased herself a yixing zisha Chinese tea set and a range of teas, which she thought might be fun to try out with the girls.

Now, she was dressed in her new, black lace camisole with a tiny black thong and strappy black sandals and ready for Caleb and David and some anal sex.

She and her ex had tried anal a few times, but although it had been an interesting feeling of stretching and fullness and certainly not painful, she'd never experienced an orgasm that way.

"Probably because in a female, the prostate gland is not next to the rectum like it is in a guy," she muttered to herself as she glanced at the clock. "In fact, it's not even called a prostate gland in a woman. It's…it's…Skene's gland," she remembered, congratulating herself as a knock came at the door.

"Caleb and David, Superior Vacations, ma'am," came a husky, sexy voice from the other side of the door.

Vivi looked through the peephole, and sure enough, there was a man with long, dark hair and deeply tanned skin and another extremely hunky man with light brown, collar-length hair. Both wore black Superior Vacations polo shirts, and the darker one carried the laptop bag.

She opened the door, and long-dark-hair said, "Hello, Vivienne, I'm Caleb."

"David," added the other one, closing the door. "I have a Prince Albert piercing I believe you're eager to see."

Vivi nodded and watched breathlessly as he kicked off his shoes and dropped his black jeans.

Commando! A long, fat cock bounced out. The piercing went in at the ridge between the stalk and the head of his cock and came out beside the eye. And at the top of the ring there was a ball.

"It will give you the most intense pleasure," said David. "Even through the condom, the jewelry will rub against your walls with every stroke, heightening the sensations, bringing you ever closer to orgasm."

Vivi felt a gush of honey flood her panties as his sexy voice and words sent shivers up and down her spine.

"Let's get you warmed up so the party can begin," added David, drawing her into his arms and rubbing his cock against her belly.

As he sent whisper-soft kisses across her forehead, she felt a pair of hands pull her thong down, then rub gently up and down her legs.

The shivers along her spine increased as warm fingers reached her butt and caressed her ass. She felt a mouth on her anus as David pulled her upper body forward and Caleb urged her to spread her legs wider. Then Caleb's lips were kissing her puckered hole, his teeth gently biting around the rim, licking and kissing as he went.

David kept kissing her face, her eyelids, her nose, her cheeks, and her earlobe, as Caleb's tongue rubbed along her slit to her clit then back to her rosette again.

Then a finger pressed cool gel into her ass as David thrust his tongue into her mouth.

More gel went into her ass as a second finger joined the first there. Then Caleb's other hand began to play with her clit.

David's hands moved to her breasts, palming them, smoothing over the rounded mounds, then reaching for her nipples. Meanwhile, his tongue was thrusting harder into her mouth.

"Push out," Caleb said as she felt a butt plug at the entry to her anus.

She did, and it slipped easily inside.

Together the men removed her camisole, which had bunched up to one side with their attentions, and gently drew her over to the bed.

They centered her on the big bed, then each took a breast in his mouth, laving, sucking, kissing, licking, until her cunt dripped steadily with honey and her head swam with need and desire.

She let her hands run through their hair—one's short and one's so long—and she realized not only that was David naked but that Caleb was wearing a lime green condom.

"I want—" she began.

"To come, darling?" asked Caleb. "Is that what you want?"

"Oh, yes, please."

"Not yet, darling. Your orgasm will be much better if you can hold off for a while. Let it build up."

David took her hand and gently sucked her fingers into his mouth, one after the other, then pressed tiny kisses to her wrist and the palm of her hand.

Caleb dropped down to her pussy and began licking and sucking her there, kissing her labia, sucking her clit, licking her slit then gently pushing his tongue on the butt plug, while David kept sucking her fingers.

Need coiled in her womb, her nerves were on fire, and Vivi pushed her hips up, desperately seeking more pressure on her clit.

"Please, I need to come," she whispered.

"Soon," soothed David, rubbing his cock ring along her thigh, making the nerves there skitter.

Caleb draped his long hair over her breasts, teasing her nipples with it, turning his head so his hair flowed over her breasts, lightly, sensitizing every inch of skin it touched.

Then David lay on his back, his head at the foot of the bed, and pulled Vivi on top of him so her cunt was level with his mouth.

"Mmmm," he hummed, sliding his tongue along her slit. "Very nice. I do like a naked pussy," he added, then sucked the edges of her labia into his mouth.

Caleb kneeled, straddling her legs, and began playing with the butt plug, gently pushing it in, twirling it around, and pulling it out a little.

With a pierced cock right by her mouth, Vivi gave in to temptation and ran her tongue around the head and over the little metal ball then licked under the ridge of David's cock, feeling the metal bars with her tongue. *Fascinating.*

She noted how he shuddered as she tongued the jewelry.

The stimulation to his cock encouraged David to lick, nibble, and gently bite her labia, causing honey to flow from Vivi's cunt and the familiar needy feeling to start gathering in her belly.

Caleb pulled the butt plug right out and squirted gel into her ass.

Where did that come from? Vivi swiveled her eyes to see the laptop bag was now on the nightstand instead of on the entertainment center.

When did they... Then Vivi's brain began to shut down as Caleb's cock started to push into her ass.

Very slowly, Caleb inched his way in, a tiny bit at a time, and Vivi could only feel. Feel the nerves around her anus tingle, her rectum open and accept the cock, her cunt dampen even more, and her belly clench with excitement.

She ran her tongue around David's cock some more, licking all over the piercing, tasting the flavor of him and his cum, noticing a slight metallic taste from the piercing.

Then her brain shut down completely as Caleb sank balls-deep in her ass and David began thrusting his tongue into her pussy.

Hands seemed to be everywhere at once, running up and down her sides, smoothing over her breasts, tugging on her nipples. Then fingers ran through her hair and started massaging her scalp.

Goose bumps spread across her skin, and she began to shudder.

Holy shit! I never knew that was sexy! Her belly clenched tighter in need.

Together the two men thrust in and out of her in perfect synchronization—in and out, gradually picking up speed and power. Fingers tweaked her nipples and pulled on them. Hands pressed over her ribs and deep into her scalp.

Her hands ran up and down firm male flesh, but she was no longer sure whose flesh she was touching. She sucked on David's cock, entranced by the feel of his Prince Albert. Both cocks were thick and stiff, drawing her closer and closer to orgasm. Then David began nibbling on her swollen and sensitive clit.

And suddenly her orgasm was there, rolling through her body with speed and power. Fingers pushed into her cunt, pressing hard on her G-spot, and she exploded into release, only just having enough presence of mind to suck hard on David's cock as she came, tipping both men over the edge and bringing them with her.

The men kissed and petted her as she came down from her orgasm, but instead of cuddling up for a nap, Caleb bundled her into the shower and washed her carefully then spread more gel in her ass while David ordered a snack from room service.

* * * *

Twenty minutes later, they were all sitting on the bed, dipping French fries into ketchup and making faces on their plates using cherry tomatoes and pieces of cheese and lettuce. They chatted about holiday destinations—places they had been, places they would like to go—and it was only as David rolled the trolley back out into the hallway after their snack that Vivi realized how truly talented and genuinely nice these men were. She could have been talking to workmates or longtime friends, the conversation had been so warm and entertaining. There was no sense at all of being with men she had just met and who had fucked her very thoroughly for a fat fee.

"Now, honey," said Caleb, running his fingers through her hair, "are you ready for the main event?"

Vivienne hesitated then nodded firmly. "Yes. Both of you at once. It's something I've wanted to try for a long time."

David reached for the Superior Vacations laptop bag again and brought out two more lime green condoms and the tube of gel. Vivi watched closely as he rolled the rubber over his Prince Albert, and sure enough, it rolled on smoothly, leaving the ball outlined but perfectly covered.

David lay on the bed and held out an arm to her. "Ride my cock, Vivi."

She crawled onto the bed and lowered herself over him, enjoying the feel of the metal sliding along her channel walls. When he was seated in her to the root, David pulled her down onto his chest so Caleb could add still more gel to her ass.

Caleb ran his fingers around the rim of her anus, exciting all the nerves there, then settled himself behind her with his knees on either side of her butt and outside David's legs and pressed his cock into her ass. It popped in past the rim then gradually slid in.

"It feels so tight, so crowded with both of you," whispered Vivi.

"You are so hot, so tight, so welcoming," breathed Caleb, "and it is so very sexy to feel each other through your wall."

When Caleb was all the way in, both men adjusted themselves so Vivi was pressed very tightly between them and their arms were around each other, forming a single unit with her as the filling in the sandwich.

David wiggled so his chest rubbed against her nipples, and Caleb flipped his hair so it teased her neck and shoulders. Then they started moving. One pushed in as the other pulled out. Very slowly, they increased the pace, in and out, still synchronized but gradually getting faster. Then harder. Their strokes became more powerful, more intense.

Vivi felt an orgasm building in her belly, then tightening, winding her higher and higher. Tension sparked in her breasts, her neck, her cunt. Her nerves tingled everywhere, from her toes to her head, sparking electrical currents throughout her.

Then the men changed pace, pulling out and pushing in together. David's Prince Albert jewelry rubbed against her pussy walls, intensifying his every movement.

With one final thrust, she felt David's cock hit her cervix, and the pleasure was so intense she screamed and shattered, her cunt spasming harder than she had ever orgasmed before. She felt David's and Caleb's cocks rubbing each other, and they, too, exploded inside her. The heat of their cum in both her channels burned into her, even through the latex. She collapsed forward onto David's chest, and he gently kissed her face, her eyelids, her forehead, whispering, "Rest now, Vivi."

She was vaguely aware of the men pulling out of her, wiping her genitals, tucking the comforter around her, then nothing.

* * * *

Once again, it was midmorning before Vivienne woke up and staggered into the hot tub. Her thigh muscles were stiff, and her ass was tender but not really sore. Still, she felt a long hot soak in the tub might be the best plan for the morning. Accompanied by a tall glass of freshly squeezed orange juice, Vivi leaned back in the tub and thought about the previous night.

"Well, I can tick another couple of questions off my list," she chatted to herself. "It is definitely pleasure, not pain, when a cock touches the cervix, but that may have been because the guy whose cock it was is very talented. And a pierced cock definitely enhances the woman's sensations during sex. And Caleb sure knew some sexy moves with his long hair. Women could borrow some of those." She giggled to herself.

Vivi leaned back, lifting her legs up onto the edges of the tub so the jets could massage her thigh muscles.

She was booked to go on a walking tour of the city's historical buildings in the afternoon, and she rather thought she might spend the evening lying by the hotel pool before having an early night. *Hmmm...Will I dine in the hotel restaurant or just have a room service snack?* She smiled at the memory of the room service snack of the evening before. *Restaurant, I think. I don't want to spoil that image.*

Chapter Three

Vivi really enjoyed wandering around the old churches and seeing the houses where some early settlers had lived. From soaring roofs, stained glass, and carved stone, to tiny rooms, humble log cabins, and simple rag rugs, it all fascinated her.

She also enjoyed poring over an extensive menu and choosing for herself without having to consider anyone else at all. It was seldom she had the freedom to do exactly as she wanted to without having to be sensible or set a good example by modeling mature behavior. Even so, she stopped at two glasses of white wine, one with a delicious chicken in lemon sauce and the other with a chocolate torte. The dry wine did not exactly go with the sweet dessert, but breaking the rules was half the fun.

The following day she spent a long time choosing a movie to see. She was so used to seeing whatever the girls wanted to see—or whatever she thought they would go and see behind her back—that it was quite hard to decide on something just for herself. Finally, she settled on a futuristic action movie and enjoyed it greatly, even though she couldn't help noticing several unexplained plot holes.

Then it was time to prepare for her evening with Eli.

* * * *

She chose to start the evening fully dressed this time, so she was wearing her favorite jeans and a feminine pale blue shirt with navy blue pumps.

Right on time, the knock came at the door, and a light tenor voice announced, "Superior Vacations, this is Eli." She checked the peephole expecting to see the regulation polo shirt, but all that was visible was a pink tongue pressed against the glass with a tongue stud centered in the viewing screen.

Giggling, she opened the door to see a delicious blond hunk with a cheeky grin and the tongue stud still very much on display. He was also carrying a bulging Superior Vacations laptop bag and wearing the expected black polo shirt and black jeans.

"Hi there, Vivienne. We're going to have so much fun this evening," said Eli. "Love those jeans. You look really hot in them. Wanna see my toys?" he asked.

Vivi nodded, but there were a few panicky feelings stirring inside her. *What if this is too much? What if I don't like the toys? What if...*

"Hey, hotstuff, don't stress. This is all about you. You can stop it at any time. I brought a pack of cards. We can play poker all night if you want," Eli rattled on. "D'ya wanna see the toys, or would you like to play cards?"

"Toys," Vivi said, drawing a deep breath. *I want this. I want to experience this. I want to know a little about BDSM.*

Eli flopped on the bed, dropping the bag beside him. "Come and sit with me and have a look," he suggested.

Vivi came over and watched while he unpacked a couple of silk scarves, a pair of fluffy pink handcuffs, a box of black condoms with different textures, a flogger with a dozen cowhide tresses and a handle that doubled as a dildo with a very realistic penis-shaped head, and a jewelry box containing nipple clamps joined by a chain and a beaded clit clamp.

Eli saw her wide-eyed stare and picked up the clit clamp. "See, it is just like tweezers with rubber tips. By twirling the metal ring, you get a perfect fit. Wanna try it?"

"Maybe the nipple ones first," gulped Vivi.

"Sure, hotstuff," replied Eli, jumping off the bed. "Let's just get you out of this pretty top first."

He stood in front of her and smoothed his hands over her breasts almost accidently as he pushed the first button through the hole to undo it. When he touched the second button, he leaned closer to her and brushed his lips lightly across hers as he released it.

By the time the final button was undone, his lips were locked to Vivi's in a passionate kiss, and his palms were pressed over her breasts, massaging them.

He thrust his tongue deep into her mouth and pressed his cock against her belly, firing her nerves up to fever pitch.

"You taste delicious, hotstuff," he whispered, moving his fingers to her back and unsnapping her bra.

His mouth moved down to her neck, pressing hot, wet kisses there, while one hand pushed her ass hard so her belly was against his engorged cock as he sucked a nipple into his mouth. Then both his hands were on her butt, squeezing and molding it, pushing her against his cock and rubbing his cock up and down her belly and lower down to her pussy. His teeth grazed her nipple, giving it tiny bites and making her groan.

Then Eli stepped away and reached for the jewelry box, leaving her hot, wet, and panting.

He attached the clamp to the nipple he had been sucking then set to work on the other one, making it as hot and engorged as the first before attaching the clamp.

"Beautiful," he breathed, and he pulled her against him for more kisses. This time he used his tongue stud to tantalize her, dragging it over her sensitive skin, licking and kissing her shoulders and breasts, then moving down her belly.

Eli dropped to his knees and undid her zipper then eased her jeans and panties down, kissing her belly and moving on down to her mons, once again dragging the tongue stud over her sensitive skin until her inner thighs were soaked and she was shivering with need.

"I'm putting the clit clamp on now, okay?" He whispered into her skin as he sucked her clit until it was standing up so he could attach the clamp.

"How does that feel, hotstuff?" he asked, looking up into her eyes, which were glazed with passion. "Oh, yeah, you like that."

Eli grabbed the beads of the clit clamp in his teeth and tugged very gently, watching Vivi shiver and shake. He wrapped an arm around her hips, pushing her cunt hard against his mouth, then drove his tongue into her channel while gently pulling on the chain of the nipple clamps with his other hand. Vivi shook even harder, and her cunt spasmed into an orgasm. Eli pushed three fingers into her pussy, curling them to press her sweet spot, then pushed the thumb of his other hand into her ass. Vivi gasped as a second, harder orgasm raced through her body, following fast on top of the first one. And if he hadn't been holding her, she was certain she would have fallen over, her legs were suddenly so wobbly.

Eli scooped her up and sat her on the end of the bed while he took her jeans, panties, and pumps all the way off, then pushed her flat onto her back while he kissed and sucked his way across her torso and on up to her breasts again.

This time he played with the chain, gently tugging it this way and that until he was sure she was on fire with need again.

"Roll over, hotstuff," he instructed, gently pushing her side.

Trembling, she obeyed, and he started kissing his way up her spine, rolling his tongue stud over her vertebrae, then reaching his hand under her body to tug on first the nipple chain, then the clit beads.

Vivi's body was flushed pink all over, she was shivering and trembling, and desperate to come.

"Fuck me, please, Eli," she begged.

"Not yet, hotstuff. Your orgasms will be much more extreme if you have to wait for a while between them. Let's raise the tension a little higher first."

He brought out the flogger and gently ran the tresses across her shoulders and back then down over her ass and thighs.

He watched her shiver and said, "Oh, yeah, hotstuff, you like that, dontcha."

Gradually, Eli moved faster and used the flogger a bit harder, until he was actually spanking her ass and upper thighs.

"Fuck me now, Eli. I need you to fuck me," she cried, desperate with want from the pleasure-pain of the flogger.

Eli flipped her over, unzipped his jeans, and pulled on one of the textured condoms almost in a single movement, then slammed his engorged cock deep into her clutching, weeping pussy.

"Yes, yes," Vivi screamed as Eli pounded into her.

"Damn, you're hot," he gasped, tilting his cock to hit her G-spot and tugging on the clit beads as Vivi shattered into orgasm. Her cunt gripped his cock like a vise and milked it so that he exploded into the condom.

Eli held her tightly as she shook with her release, then removed all the clamps and sucked first her nipples, then her clit to help the blood flow back into them.

They lay side by side for a few minutes. Then Eli bounced off the bed, grabbing her hand to pull her up.

"Come on. Let's have a shower," he said.

She was so sated and limp after her orgasm, Eli had to pull and coax Vivi into the bathroom. He leaned her against the wall while he adjusted the spray and water temperature. Then he placed her right in the center of the cubicle. He left her there for a moment then returned with a handful of bottles, which he dumped on the shelf.

"Lean against the wall, hotsuff," he said, pushing her toward the back of the shower recess. After she obeyed him, he poured lotions onto her shoulders and massaged them, then smoothed the bubbles down her back, rubbing and soothing her tired muscles, massaging her butt, and continuing down her legs, soaping and soothing as he went.

Finally, he turned her around and repeated his ministrations down over her arms, her breasts, her tummy, to her legs, and even her toes. Every inch of her was gently soaped, massaged, and soothed, until her body was completely relaxed and cosseted by his caring touch. He patted her dry on the huge fluffy towel provided by the hotel then carried her back to the bed, lying her on her side and spooning himself in behind her.

"Rest now for a little while, hotstuff," he whispered, and she soon drifted off to sleep.

* * * *

An hour so later, Vivi woke to find herself flat on her back, handcuffed to the headboard, her eyes blindfolded—with one of the scarves, maybe?—and something soft but arousing being dragged over her belly.

"I thought you'd like that, hotsuff," said the light tenor voice with a hint of a grin in it.

"Mmmm," was all Vivi could manage to say as the soft fabric swirled over her breasts and stomach then down her legs, and her skin started to tingle.

As Eli continued to tantalize her, Vivi decided it must be the flogger tresses he was using, but they somehow felt different from earlier that evening.

"See how the blindfold works, hotstuff? When one sense is taken away, all the others are heightened, and the skin is the most erogenous zone of them all."

Vivi nodded then gasped as he licked along her slit and then sucked her clit into his mouth. Then the clamp was on her clit again, and his tongue was in her channel, sliding along her walls and thrusting deep inside.

Vivi tried to lift off the bed but was stopped by the handcuffs through the headboard. Her arms tensed, then she deliberately relaxed them and forced herself to concentrate on the intense sensations she could feel. Her brain was screaming for her to get the blindfold off so she could see what he was doing to her, but she ignored it.

"Relax, hotsuff. Taste yourself on me."

And Eli's tongue was in her mouth. Vivi relaxed into the experience. Her juices were a little salty and tart, but it wasn't an unpleasant taste, and it was surprisingly arousing, erotic.

"Do you lick your fingers after you pleasure yourself?" he asked, peppering kisses along her jaw line and across to her earlobe.

"Yes. Once or twice I tried it. But it just seemed a weird thing to do. On you it is—different. Sexy. Hot," she replied.

"Oh, you're definitely hot, honey. Why d'you think I've been calling you hotstuff? Your breasts are full and round. Just the right size for a man to hold," he said, suiting the action to the words. Then he tweaked her nipples saying, "Your nipples are like hard little berries reaching up for my mouth like the fruit reaches up into the sunlight. Your belly is just a little rounded, as are your hips. Perfect to hold as I fuck you. No man wants to hold a bag of bones. Real men want real women in their beds."

He bent and licked her bellybutton then kissed his way down to her mons. "Your cunt lips are swollen and pink, and your clit looks delicious with the clamp on it."

He tugged on the beads gently, and honey seeped from her channel.

His sexy talk combined with the kisses and touching was making desire curl in her core again. And not being able to see him, to know what he was looking at or about to touch next, was adding to the fire in her belly.

Something hard and warm nudged into her cunt, slid down her channel. Filled her. It was not his cock. And she had not seen a dildo in the laptop bag.

Wait.

The handle of the flogger. That's what it was, the penis-shaped handle of the flogger.

Eli moved the handle in and out, from side to side, up and down, in figure eights. Vivi started to move her hips. It was good, but she needed more.

Then her legs were pushed back toward her chest by a strong arm, the dildo stopped moving, and a cool gel was squirted into her anus.

"Eli, what—"

"Oh, you know what's going to happen next, hotstuff. I'm going to fuck your ass while my plastic friend here fucks your cunt. And let me just get these nipple clamps back on. We wouldn't want those luscious nipples to miss out on all the fun, would we?"

He lowered her legs and put her feet flat on the bed with her knees wide apart, sucked each nipple hard, then set the clamps in place, twirling the dildo from time to time to keep her cunt hungry for more. Then he slid his fingers into her ass, scissoring them, moving them around, stretching her tissues, and making her yearn for more than just fingers in her dark passage.

By the time his cock was in her rectum, she was on fire with need, and little tugs from him on the nipple chain, the clit beads, and the handle of the flogger had her brain frying trying to guess what he would tease next.

"Take the blindfold off. I want to see you. I want to see what is happening," Vivi begged.

"Okay, hotstuff, just for you."

Still with his cock lodged firmly in her ass, Eli leaned forward along her body, pressing hard on her sensitive breasts and sending streaks of pleasure-pain from her nipples to her cunt. He pulled off the blindfold—yes, it was one of the silk scarves as she'd thought—and unhooked the handcuffs from the headboard, freeing her wrists. While Vivienne was still blinking as her eyes adjusted to the light after being covered, he rubbed her wrists and shoulders to make sure the blood was flowing through them properly.

Almost before she was aware of what was happening, he thrust deep into her ass and began moving the dildo in circles inside her cunt again, shifting his other hand from her hip, to her breasts, to her clit in a random pattern that had her totally on edge wondering what he would touch next.

Vivi grabbed his shoulders and hung onto him as the sensations curled in her belly, tightening and strengthening with his every thrust in her ass. His hands seemed to be everywhere at once, twirling the dildo in her pussy, tugging on the nipple clamps' chain and the clit beads, smoothing over her arms, her breasts, even her spine.

He thrust hard and deep into her ass with his cock, leaning forward and using his pelvis to push the dildo in as far into her cunt as it would go, then held her head with both his hands and thrust his tongue into her mouth, using his tongue stud to tease the insides of her cheeks. Vivi felt her orgasm explode over her, seeming to come from her breasts, her clit, her mouth, and her belly all at once. Waves of fire flashed through her body as it convulsed in passion. She felt Eli's cock jerk and twitch in her ass and knew he'd come, too, as he thrust a few more times to extend her orgasm.

Then, still with his cock buried in her, he undid the clamps, sucking her nipples once more before feathering a few more kisses across her breasts.

He slid out of her ass, removed the flogger from her pussy, and undid the clit clamp, sucking on her clit one last time to soothe it.

Then he rubbed some lavender oil into her wrists, shoulders, breasts, and over her clit, dripping some gel into her ass, and tucking her under the comforter.

"Enjoy your vacation, hotstuff," he whispered into her ear.

"Thank you," she mumbled, drifting into sleep.

Chapter Four

Vivienne was tired of spending most of her time in the city, so she hired a car to drive out to the beach. It was about a two-hour drive, which gave her plenty of time to think over all her new experiences of the past week. She'd seen and done a lot of things she'd only heard the kids talk about. And she was awed by the powerful orgasms the men had given her. "I guess that is the best thing about having a professional to show me." She giggled to herself. Each of the men had been quite different, and although she'd only spent a night with each one, she had sensed unique personalities to each of them.

Vivi spent several miles trying to decide if Eli had made such a deep impression on her because he was different from the others or because he was alone and not accompanied by a partner as the other men had been. Her first glimpse of the sea through a gap in the trees drew her mind from him and onto her plans for the day.

She'd bought a sandwich and some fruit plus several bottles of water from the snack bar at the hotel, had a romance novel with her to read, and wore the obligatory hat and sunscreen, so she was prepared to stay until dark.

The clerk at the car hire desk had given her good advice. The beach was a "family friendly" one, which meant that as a lone female, she was safe there. But since school was in and it was midweek, the sand was not cluttered with kids running around screaming and shouting. People were lying on blankets or sitting on beach chairs far enough apart for some privacy, but not so distant as to provide a target for thieves or perverts.

The golden sand was pristine, the water a deep blue-green, and the sky a clear blue. The sun was warm enough to make sitting on a towel in her bikini a pleasure and a swim cool and refreshing.

Vivi stripped off her skirt and T-shirt, plopped her sunhat over her long brown curls, and stretched out on her towel with her book, ready to soak in the sun and relax.

Later, she walked out into the water until she was chest-deep then swam parallel with the shore up and back the length of the beach half a dozen times, floated on her back for a while, and lay on the sand in the shallows.

She ate her meal, drank some water, read her book, and finally, as darkness began to fall, headed back to the hotel, feeling refreshed, rejuvenated, and somehow much clearer in her mind about what she wanted to do with her life from now on.

* * * *

Vivienne stood at her closet, undecided about what to wear for her final night of sex. Frank and George. Originally she'd planned to be wearing just a lacy, caramel camisole and thong set, which would enhance the faintly sun-kissed color of her skin after her day at the beach yesterday. But then she thought maybe she should wear a dress, which meant wearing a bra instead of the camisole.

What does it matter what I wear? I'll be naked soon enough. But somehow it did matter. For some unknown reason, it was important.

With just five minutes until the men were to arrive according to the clock on the entertainment center, Vivi flipped a coin. "Heads a dress, tails underwear," she called as the coin spun in the air. Heads. Vivi slid into a sunshine-yellow dress just moments before the knock came on her door.

Frank was slightly taller, slightly heavier, and slightly darker in skin and hair color than George, but they were both well built and heavily muscled. Very strong-looking men. And they were going to fuck each other while she watched. Vivi had heard several girls say it was the sexiest thing they'd ever seen, and Vivi knew men liked to watch two women fucking, so the idea made sense to her. But she wanted to experience it herself.

George moved the chair away from the desk, placing it where anyone on it would have an uninterrupted view of the carpeted area and also of the bed. "Sit over here, Vivienne, and the show will begin," he said, gesturing for her to move to the chair.

Silently, Vivi nodded, and the two men came together. Staring into each other's eyes and grinding their pelvises together, Frank and George began undressing each other. Vivi found herself breathing harder as polo shirts were wrenched over heads, shoes were kicked off, and jeans were tugged down muscular thighs.

After a few moments of frantic activity, both men's thongs were revealed, Frank's a tiny leopard print and George's black and studded. Frank grabbed George's hair and pulled him closer, pressing his lips to the other man's in a passionate kiss. There was nothing gentle about it. Tongues dueled and teeth clashed together. Their hips ground together, and George's hand slid over Frank's butt and into the crack, so Vivi had no doubt that a finger or two had plunged into his rectum.

Their cocks had swollen hugely now and strained to escape from their thongs. George pressed his pelvis and the studded thong hard into Frank, rubbing his cock up and down, and Vivi could imagine how the studs would feel digging into all that hot flesh.

Looking at the bulging packages, Vivi felt her own thong grow damp and her cunt clench with the need to feel one of those cocks inside her—a feeling only heightened and intensified when the men stripped their thongs off and the cocks bounced free. George's was very long and Frank's extremely wide.

Frank wrapped his hand around both cocks and, holding them together, rubbed up and down until Vivi could see pre-cum pearling in the tips of both. George maneuvered the men over to where the laptop bag was lying on the entertainment center, opened it one-handed, rummaged through the contents, and came out holding a string of condoms.

Without saying a word or even seeming to give each other a sign, the men backed onto the bed, Frank dropped onto his back and lifted his legs up high and wide while George sheathed himself, and without any preparation other than the quick touch Vivi assumed had happened a few moments before, George plunged straight into Frank's ass right to the hilt. George tilted Frank's hips up and began a punishingly fast plunge and retreat while Frank's hand gripped his cock, stroking it in the same rhythm.

George leaned forward and began sucking and biting at one of Frank's nipples, and Frank used his other hand to pinch George's nipple.

Vivi's eyes were wide open, her breath was coming fast, and a hand slid under her dress and into her panties to touch her clit.

The men's bodies slammed together in a wild display of raw power, and Vivi plunged her fingers into her cunt, groaning right along with them. Frank's cock erupted into spurts of white semen over both men's groins, George gave one last thrust into Franks' ass, and Vivi came right along with them.

The men disappeared into the bathroom, and Vivi was left hot and shaking from what she had watched.

"You liked that, didn't you?" asked George when he came back into the room.

"I've never seen anything so hot before," she replied.

"Oh, you will, you will. Give us a few moments to recover, and we'll make you very hot indeed."

Frank came out of the bathroom saying, "The hot tub is on and filling up. Let me just grab some supplies, and what do you say we move this party into the hot tub?"

"Good plan," said George, helping Vivi out of her chair and leading her into the other room.

While Frank put the laptop bag in easy reach of the tub and tipped bubbles and scented bath oil into the water, George drew Vivi into his arms and gently kissed her lips. Then with hands so slow and gentle and completely different from the raw scene of a few moments ago, he unzipped her dress and helped her out of it. As he kissed the sensitive place where her neck and shoulders joined, Frank moved behind her and unfastened her bra. George's mouth moved down to kiss the hollow of her throat, and his hands slid over her shoulders, pushing the bra strap off her arms and dropping it to the floor.

Meanwhile, Frank pulled her thong down her legs then off over her feet. George turned her slightly so she could watch Frank hold the scrap of lace up to his nose and inhale deeply. Vivi blushed as Frank said, "Delicious."

The men settled her in the tub with her leaning back against the side and themselves cross-legged in front of her.

Frank took her hand in his and smoothed circles across her palm with his thumb then lifted her wrist to his mouth and kissed it. Slowly, he sucked one finger after the other into his mouth, sucking firmly on each one before letting it go and sucking in the next one.

Vivi was surprised to feel her stomach muscles clench at the promise in his eyes of what else he would be kissing and sucking just like this, but later.

Meanwhile, George picked up her foot and mimicked Frank's motions with her toes. Vivi's heart beat faster as the men trailed their fingers along her skin, one up her arm and the other up her leg. Two male heads bent and placed soft butterfly kisses along her limbs, and Vivi's breathing hitched as need coiled tight inside her and her pulse rate accelerated even further.

Just when she was expecting fingers or even a cock in her pussy, the men let go of her and moved back to the other side of the tub.

"W-What? I would have come the moment you entered me," she said.

"That's the whole point, Vivi," explained Frank. "The longer you hold off having an orgasm, the higher you will fly when you eventually come. Each time we build you up toward release, you will start off from a higher place and go still farther. When you finally climax, it will be the best orgasm you've ever had."

"Guaranteed," added George.

Oh, yes. Eli said that, too. And someone else. Caleb, maybe? Or David?

And the men proceeded to lean back in the tub and talk to Vivi about everyday things.

Five minutes later, they resumed their touching and caressing, and just as they had promised, she was instantly hot, wet, and needy. This time, they each took a breast, kissing, licking, sucking, teasing the slopes of her globes and then the nipples. But once again, when she was on the brink of coming, they moved away.

They repeated the procedure a third time, and then when they came to her the fourth time, she grabbed a handful of each man's hair and said, "So help me, if you don't fuck me this time, you'll both be bald!"

Laughing, they flipped her against the side of the tub, pressing her cunt over the jet so the bubbles hit her right on the clit, then they proceeded to tease and stretch her anus, to play with her pussy lips, and to slide their fingers inside her cunt. But they never gave her enough to let her come.

Vivi was shaking and sobbing with need when Frank sat in the center of the tub, slid a condom on his wide, fat cock, then pulled her down over it, sliding deep inside her, stretching her walls and making her sigh with the relief of being filled.

Meanwhile, George slathered his condom-covered cock with waterproof lube and squeezed more of it into her ass as Frank held her tilted onto his chest, his cock still firmly ensconced inside her pussy.

Then George pushed past the tight ring of anal muscles and into the hot depths of her rectum. Frank held very still while George worked his way right inside, and Vivi reveled in the hot, tight feeling of being full to bursting with two cocks.

Very slowly, they started to move inside her, occasionally kissing her neck, shoulders, breasts, or lips, sometimes touching her ribs or breasts or nipples, but always stopping before she reached a peak. Gradually, the men moved a little faster, a little harder, touched her more purposefully, while Vivi thrashed and moaned, desperate for release. Finally, they both plunged hard into her, slamming to the hilt, and two hands pinched her nipples. With a long, loud scream, Vivi came, shaking so hard she thought her bones would break, in an orgasm that powered through her for what seemed like minutes. Her toes curled, her entire body shook like a tree in a storm, and Vivi almost passed out under the intense pleasure.

She recovered to find herself being held by one man and patted dry with a big, fluffy towel by the other. Then she was carried into the bedroom and tucked under the comforter, and two men pressed kisses to her eyelids, saying, "Sleep now. You've earned it."

* * * *

When Vivi woke late that morning, it was to find no evidence of the night before. And she realized there never had been. Each morning when she'd awoken, the room had been spotless. No discarded condoms or empty tubes of lube. No towels dropped on the floor. Her room was always left perfectly neat, so she almost might have imagined the night before, except for a certain amount of soreness in various overworked but oh-so-grateful muscles.

* * * *

Later, sitting in the restaurant eating a delayed but delicious breakfast, Vivi acknowledged she'd come to some decisions about her life over this past week. She would go ahead with a piercing, but of her bellybutton, not her nipple. She wanted something she could display to friends as a sign of this vacation. A visible symbol of the emotional progress she'd made.

And she would look for a man to form a relationship with. Maybe just a fuck buddy, but maybe also someone she could talk with and share her life with. Or maybe two men—one for fucking and one for talking.

Whomever she met, she knew that she'd passed some kind of test and was ready to really live her life from now on, not just to watch life pass her by.

Vivi raised her glass of orange juice in a toast. "To Adam, Ben, Caleb, David, Eli, Frank, and George. You wonderful men gave me a truly superior vacation, and I thank you all from the bottom of my heart."

PART II

Chapter Five

Vivi sighed and stared at the faces of the teenagers sitting with her around the dining table in their shared house. She had a new batch of young women and was trying to teach them the basics of budgeting and cooking cheap, nutritious meals. All of them were stick-thin, and every one of them was terrified of gaining an ounce of weight.

"I understand all that, but if you want to be healthy, you need to get a certain level of nutrients each day. Taking a stack of multivitamin pills will do that, but it's quite expensive and can be a worry, as taking some pills make other pills not work properly and can even make you sick." Vivi looked at the young faces again and was relieved to see at least some of the girls nodding.

"So a much cheaper and safer way of getting the nutrition you need is to eat one meal every day that's got a lot of the vitamins you need in it, and I can teach you some recipes that will do that. Also, we can make up a batch of recipes one day a week and freeze them in meal-sized servings, so you only need to grab a box out of the freezer and put it in the microwave for a few minutes, and you're good for the day, all the rest of the week."

"But won't we need to buy all sorts of fancy stuff at the store to do that?" asked Rylee, a sixteen-year-old Vivienne hoped would return to school next semester. She was a bright girl and deserved a chance to pass enough classes to graduate.

"Not necessarily. Pasta, rice, vegetables, and some lean meat are what we need. We have a range of herbs and spices here in the pantry and can add a few shakes of this and that if you want to."

Vivi dropped a pile of recipes into the center of the table and watched the young women start to look at them and become animated. They really were quite good kids. They simply needed someone to give them a gentle push in the right direction.

Sitting next to Rylee was Mikayla, another sixteen-year-old, but one who had seen far too much of life thanks to an abusive family situation.

Chloe, Payton, and Genesis sat on the opposite side of the table—all seventeen and not one of them with the literacy and numeracy skills of an average fourth grader. The hardest part of teaching them to cook would be getting them to understand the words and quantities involved in even simple recipes. Teaching them to budget was going to be even trickier. Thank God they all had cell phones with a calculator function.

At the end of the table was Neveah. A tiny little thing, she was supposedly fifteen, but Vivi doubted that. Still, with regular meals and a safe place to sleep, maybe she'd grow some and talk a little more, too. Vivi wasn't sure about her story, but she was willing to bet it hadn't included much time at school or guidance in life skills.

Nice kids, but this batch is gonna be a hell of a lot of work!

* * * *

Vivi's job required her to be on call for the young women in her care 24/7, but once a month, a relief couple moved into the house, and she had four days and nights of freedom either in a place of her own choosing or in one of the apartments provided by the organization that employed her.

A new charity had recently been established where troubled young people would live on a farm out in the country, a long way from any town, and learn how to get their lives back on track after recovering from addictions, abuse, or leaving the juvenile justice system. Vivi had been offered the chance to spend her four days off there this month and was excited at meeting colleagues and seeing new possibilities for "her" kids.

It was only a four-hour drive, but the property was not signposted—deliberately, Vivi guessed—and instructions like "the third track on the right about ten miles from the T intersection" were not all that helpful.

"Dammit, is that the road I need or just someone's driveway?" cursed Vivi as she drove slowly past a pair of gates. Another mile on, with no more potential tracks, Vivi realized she should have turned and had to travel yet another mile before the one-lane road was wide enough for her to safely turn a one eighty and go back.

Once through the gates, Vivi drove slowly along a narrow dirt track for what seemed like forever but was probably only another couple of miles until she passed a tumbled-down shack, which was her signal to go to the right.

She'd followed a pair of barely visible wheel ruts for maybe a mile when she crested a low hill and a large house came into view. It looked very pretty, with a lake on one side of it and a large barn on the other. Neat vegetable gardens were laid out behind the house, and rows of fruit trees were farther back still.

Vivi drove down the hill and into a courtyard area in front of the house. A wide-roofed porch had comfy chairs, a porch-swing, and several small tables on it. And standing up from one of the chairs was the yummiest man Vivi had seen in a very long time. Such a shame he was way too young for her, though. He had to be twelve or fifteen years younger than she, at least six feet tall, and a solid wall of muscle from the clearly defined calves underneath his knee-length shorts to the top of his shaggy black hair that was just begging her to run her fingers through it.

Unbuckling her seatbelt, Vivienne glanced in the rearview mirror to check she wasn't drooling before opening her car door and climbing out.

Mr. Yummilicious bounced down the porch steps and extended his hand to her. A big, strong, tanned hand with sturdy fingers that enveloped her smaller hand infused her with a heat that soaked right through to her bones.

"Vivienne Carstairs? I'm Ryan Elliott. My *partner*, Boyd Williams, and I have been looking forward to your visit. We want to show you all around the property and hope our venture will help you in your work."

Partner! Well, damn! They way he said that word it can only mean one thing. Why are all the best-looking ones always gay! And just when I'm ready for some sexy action and he makes every one of my cylinders rev right up, too.

Vivi dragged her mind back to the present and her hand out of his clasp. "Hi, Ryan. Good to meet you. The program you've got here sounds really interesting. I'm looking forward to everything you'll show me." *Damn, that sounds a bit double entendre-ish! Get your mind out of his pants, woman!*

But she couldn't miss seeing the rather large package he had tucked inside those long shorts. Or the muscles rippling across his chest under the tight T-shirt he wore. Not to mention the ones in his arms as he gathered her luggage and easily lifted it up the steps onto the porch.

The house was large and rambling, like so many old buildings, with hallways and rooms leading off at odd angles with no apparent logic, but it still had an aura of warm welcome. The polished hardwood floors shone, bright, cheery rugs were scattered here and there, and the living area included a circle of deep, soft, squishy armchairs.

The kitchen gleamed with modern appliances and was presided over by a smiling, middle-aged woman with gray hair, twinkling blue eyes, and an ample waistline hidden behind a crisp white apron. "Call me Molly, dear. Coffee is always hot, those muffins are just out of the oven this morning, and there's plenty of fresh fruit in that bowl," she said, waving her hand at the various items as she mentioned them.

"Thanks, Molly. When I've put my luggage away, I'll be back for some of your coffee. And a muffin," she added, seeing how much Ryan was enjoying the one he'd snagged off the platter.

"The north wing is for the guys, and their bathroom and bedrooms are over there. The girls are all in the south wing," said Ryan, heading to the lake side of the house. "The living areas with the kitchen and dining room are in the middle. Boyd and I have our rooms at the front of the house with the business office."

Ryan stopped at one of the rooms. "We're trying to establish trust here. The door has a bolt, so you can bolt yourself inside if you wish. The desk drawer has a lock, so you can put your valuables in there. But we don't have security cameras or external locks on the rooms. The pantry is never locked. Non-prescription drugs, tobacco, and alcohol are absolutely banned on the property—all the property not just inside the house. But if someone wants to leave, they are free to do so. However, should they choose to leave, for many of them it means they forfeit their chances of assisted rehabilitation and will have to go it alone. Integrating back into society, finding a job, supporting yourself without advice and help is tough. But if the young people make that choice, we're not going to stop them or report them to the authorities."

"Yes, I noticed there wasn't even a cattle grid on the track in here. I wondered how you'd stop someone driving off."

"We lock our own cars, but the tractor and other farm equipment keys are hanging on a hook in the office, so anyone can access them as they need. It's all about building trust, responsibility, and self-esteem. Anyway, we'll talk about all that later, and at length. For now, unpack your suitcase, have your coffee, then come back to the living room, and I'll take you around the rest of the property and show you what we're attempting to do here."

* * * *

Vivi unpacked her small suitcase, feeling grateful that she didn't smoke and could live without alcohol. In fact, the rules were similar to those in the house she ran. Their aim was to build into the young people self-confidence and a sense of self-esteem, and that was better achieved without using crutches like hard or soft drugs.

And just looking at Ryan was giving her a buzz much stronger than one she'd get from a glass of wine, anyway.

"I wonder what the other man, Boyd, looks like?" she mused as she put her underwear in the chest of drawers. "Lucky I brought my swimsuit. That was a fluke, but the lake looks pretty, and the weather is warm enough at the moment to swim." For a brief second, she rested her hand on her bellybutton, feeling the little heart jewel she had on her piercing.

Vivi placed her empty luggage in the closet, locked her purse in the desk drawer, tucked her pajamas neatly under the pillow, then walked back to the kitchen.

A gangling youth of some seventeen years was sitting at the big table, three muffins on a plate in front of him and a huge glass of milk in his hand. He swallowed hastily, bobbed his head, and mumbled, "Hi, I'm Freddy," before taking another gulp from his milk.

"Hi, Freddy. My name's Vivienne. I'm here for a few days to look around."

"Yeah, Boyd said you were coming. I'm learning all about fruit trees. You treat an apple tree quite different from a grapefruit tree, ya know. I'll take you out on the tractor and show you tomorrow, if you'd like," he said earnestly before shoving half a muffin into his mouth.

"I'd like that very much. I don't know much about fruit trees at all. What other trees do you have?"

Vivi filled a mug with coffee from the pot, took a plate and a muffin, and sat beside Freddy as he talked about the orchard. As well as three different types of apple trees and the grapefruit, they had oranges, apricots, and macadamia nut trees and were planning to extend the orchard and try out some more varieties of trees.

Freddy gulped the last of his milk, took his glass and plate over to the sink, thanked Molly, nodded to Vivi, and loped back outside. Vivi finished her coffee then copied his actions before going back to the living room to meet up with Ryan.

Vivi paused on the threshold of the living room as her breath caught in her throat. Ryan might be Mr. Yummilicious personified, but the man who was standing beside him, likely Boyd, was Mr. Sex on a Stick. Maybe an inch or so shorter than Ryan's six foot plus, this man was a little leaner but with defined muscles, very fair hair, and light blue eyes sparkling out of a tanned face and framed by the crinkles of laugh lines stretching from the corners of his eyes almost to his ears.

His very kissable lips were curved up in a delightful smile, and the potency of him had Vivi's panties dampening and her belly clenching with desire. *And at least a dozen years younger than me, damn it all to hell! Not to mention Ryan's partner.*

Mr. Sex on a Stick rushed over to her, took her hand between his, and stared deeply into her eyes. "You must be Vivienne. I'm Boyd," he stated in a deep, rumbly bass voice that sent a fresh rush of cream pouring from her pussy onto her already damp panties.

Vivi took a deep breath, slid her hand out from his, and tried to slow down her pounding heart and gather her lust-scattered wits enough to answer like a mature woman instead of a sex-starved nymphomaniac.

"Hi, Boyd. Yes, I'm Vivi, and I'm very interested in the program you and Ryan are running here." *I'd rather jump into bed with both of you and fuck your brains out, but since you are partners and much younger than me, I'll try to get a grip on my hormones!*

Boyd led her across the room to a chair between him and Ryan and began explaining the program. Soon, Vivi had controlled her lust and was genuinely and excitedly intrigued with the farm's potential for the young people she worked with.

Several hours passed as Vivi asked questions and the men went into greater and greater detail. "This is awesome. I so want my girls to participate. To get them out of the city, out into the sunshine and fresh air, learning new skills, and away from so many temptations. For them to stay long enough in one home to plant seeds and watch them grow. So many of these kids have been shunted from place to place with no stability in their lives. Being here for six months would be so good for them."

"If they want to, they could stay twelve months and achieve a certificate in horticulture. If that doesn't interest them, we have some other options, too, such as small engine mechanics. The literacy and numeracy programs are also useful. We've found a lot of these young people have had very sporadic school attendance."

Vivi nodded as Ryan spoke.

"Yes," she said, "when your home life is unstable, attending school becomes a low priority. Some of the girls I have with me at the moment are well behind in their education, and that is pretty much normal for the kids I see."

Vivi leaned back in her chair and became aware of the sounds of voices calling and feet stomping in the old farmhouse. She raised a questioning eyebrow at Boyd. He smiled in response.

"Ah, yes. The boys are never late for supper. And Molly is a stickler for clean hands and fingernails. She sends them back to the bathroom to scrub again if she isn't satisfied. They soon learn to arrive in time for a proper shower before the meal."

Vivi laughed then looked at her own fingernails. "Think I'll pass?"

Ryan stepped across the small distance from his chair to hers. He gently drew her to her feet and then carefully inspected her hands. "Perfect," he whispered, dropping a light kiss on her knuckles.

All the lust that had been buried underneath her enthusiasm for this project suddenly exploded like molten lava from a volcano. Her belly clenched, her nipples hardened, her heart began to pound. In vain, she reminded herself that these men were partnered to each other, but her body wasn't listening. Her body was screaming, "Fuck me!"

Suddenly, her brain stopped functioning, too. Before she could stop herself, her mouth opened, and she asked, "So, Boyd and Ryan, you are partners? You are together?"

Fiery heat flamed across her face, and she clapped her hands to her mouth in dismay. But the men both laughed.

"Oh, yes, Vivi. We are together. We have loved each other for three years now, and we've been living and working together almost all that time," said Ryan.

"But we are bisexual," added Boyd. "At first we used to go out occasionally and have a woman each because we enjoy women, as well. However, once we became committed partners, it seemed like being unfaithful, so these days we like to share a woman."

"One day we hope to find one we both like who would be interested in a ménage relationship. Have you ever had two men?" asked Ryan.

Vivi's blush deepened. Now her whole body felt hot, not just her face. Nevertheless, she nodded. There was no way she would tell these two attractive younger men about her vacation, but she did need to let them know she was interested in them. Very, very interested in them.

"Yes, I have. It was the best orgasm I've ever experienced in my life."

The atmosphere in the room was thick with lust. It burned from Boyd's light blue eyes as he glanced from Vivi to Ryan, and from Ryan's chocolate brown ones as he returned the look.

A bell rang at the back of the house, and the voices of many young people called out.

Vivi glanced at the men and breathed deeply, willing her flushed body to calm down.

"Supper," the men said together. "Let's go."

* * * *

The meal was noisy and chaotic, but Vivi enjoyed herself, gradually putting names to the young people around her, listening intently to their conversation and joining in from time to time.

Their manners were a little rough, and their language tended to be coarse, but she could see the way so many of them idolized Molly, and she was impressed. She was even more impressed when Freddy came over to her after a dessert of delicious apple crumble and said, "I'll be out in the orchard at ten tomorrow. If you meet me outside the barn, I'll show you around."

"Thank you, Freddy. I'd really like that." And she realized she was looking forward to it and to getting to know this young man better and seeing him display his skills.

After the meal, most of the young men went outside for a ball game on the grass. She had no idea what they were playing, but they formed two teams simply by half of them taking their shirts off, and the game seemed to involve running madly from one end of the yard to the other, with or without the ball.

She relaxed on the porch with a few of the boys and let her eyes roam over Boyd and Ryan, who were on opposing teams. Ryan's shirtless torso was more drool-worthy than she had even imagined, and her fantasies ran wild, beginning with the three of them in bed together. *Not going to happen with a houseful of young men and women to watch every move and hear every noise.*

The half-dozen girls in the project then came out on the grass and joined in, all of them displaying an excellent understanding of the game and none taking their shirts off despite splitting themselves evenly between the teams. One little redhead also had a real sense of where the ball was going to end up, and time and time again she was in the right place at the right time.

"That's Rhiannon," said a soft voice beside Vivienne. "She used to train with the state athletics team."

Vivi turned to smile at the boy beside her. "She is very, very good. Is she going to try out for a college team?"

His face fell. "Well, our teacher, Andy, hopes she'll be able to go back to high school at the start of next year, but then she'll have to catch up on a lot of subjects. Boyd said she might be able to get some extra teaching, but…"

"If she wants to go back to school, I'm sure Boyd and Ryan will get help for her. What about you? You're Peter, aren't you? What do you want to do?"

Peter brightened again and spoke about his desire to work with animals.

Gradually, the daylight faded, the game ended, and the young adults all came inside again to watch TV, play computer games, and head off to bed. Vivi noticed Molly had left a giant basket of fruit out and that many of the boys took some with them to their rooms.

Just goes to show that if takeout doesn't deliver, kids will eat healthy. I do hope my girls can join a project like this.

Chapter Six

Vivi ran her hands down her sides. She was dressed in her sober, navy blue, one-piece swimsuit, her bellybutton piercing hidden from sight. This afternoon, everyone was meeting at the lake, and one of the instructors, Basil, was going to teach anyone who wanted to learn how to do an Eskimo roll in a kayak.

An Eskimo roll sounded like some weird kind of ice cream or cookie to her, but apparently it was some tricky maneuver to prevent a kayaker from drowning.

The previous few days had passed quickly, filled to the brim with talking to the people at the farmhouse, wandering around looking at the various projects, and lusting after Ryan and Boyd. Vivi was almost certain they wanted her, too, but of course nothing could happen on-site. Although logic suggested that since the men lived there surely they must…

Vivi stayed safely on the shore while Basil demonstrated an Eskimo roll. The idea was to turn the kayak from an upright position laterally 360 degrees—going underwater and coming back up—while still moving forward. It looked so easy when Basil did it, but it was obviously a lot trickier to do than it appeared. A group of eager young men volunteered to attempt it first, and most of them ended up in the water out of their kayaks. Some managed to stay in the kayak, but not one managed to get it upright again, much less while moving forward.

After hours of trying and laughing, it was Freddy who was the first to succeed. A horde of young adults ran splashily to him to hug him and congratulate him. Then they dunked him.

Immediately, it became a free-for-all playtime with fountains of water flying everywhere.

Ryan, Boyd, and Basil hastily got out of the water while the younger onlookers rushed in to join the fun.

Vivi stayed nice and dry on the sidelines, laughing as these troubled young people, who often seemed so much older than their years and who had lived through things adults should never have to experience, were enjoying being young and free in the sunshine and water.

"It's so good to see them enjoying life," she said to the men. Then her breath caught and heart started to pound as she looked at Boyd and Ryan. Both of them so tall and muscular and Ryan so gloriously tanned. Boyd was all bright lightness, leaner and sleeker than Ryan and looking like an extremely sexy fish with droplets of water on his toned muscles. Sex on a Stick times two.

Boyd's eyes were crinkled with laughter. Ryan's broad shoulders gleamed in the sunlight. Their muscles were defined, their asses taut inside their board shorts.

She was getting to know the two men better, too. Just talking to them, they didn't seem young, but when she looked at their faces, she knew the dozen or more years between them were another barrier to any possible relationship. People would talk about an old lady of forty-one partnering with young men of less than thirty. Besides, she was sure once she really got to know them, generational differences would appear to crack the possibility of a relationship. Not to mention they already had each other and had only mentioned a woman for an occasional ménage.

As the hilarity died down, the men organized some swimming races and competitions, and Vivi participated with the girls, the afternoon passing so swiftly she hardly had time to comprehend that tomorrow she would be going back to work.

* * * *

Early the next morning, both men were out on the porch to wish her a safe trip back home.

"I'll be asking for permission to bring the girls here for six months. This program is just what they need," she said.

"And we'll be visiting you next month when we come into the city to make our quarterly report," Ryan replied with such a lustful look in his eyes Vivi could not help but imagine what was in their minds. It was in hers, too.

Hardly a day went by without a phone call or email or both from either Ryan or Boyd. Vivi looked forward to their conversations. It was more than just lust, a hope for sex which she was not sure would ever eventuate. They were becoming friends. They understood each other, had so much of the same view of life, and felt so similar about their respective jobs that Ryan and Boyd were almost like an extension of herself.

The organization she worked for was enthusiastic about the potential of the farm to give young people a new focus and direction. Vivi had been called into the city three times now to meet with the board of directors and talk about the time she had spent there, the programs she had seen running, the young people she had spent time with, and the type of input she would be able to make if the girls in her care went there for six months. Vivi felt confident that such a trial would be forthcoming.

She also felt hopeful about spending the night with Ryan and Boyd when they came to the city. Nothing had been said, no words of love, lust, or sex had been mentioned, but tenderness and care were part of their vocabulary, and she believed their relationship would progress, even though she was not sure how that would work if she was to spend six months at the farm.

Did Boyd and Ryan sleep together at the farm, or only when they were on leave? Could she work beside them day after day, week after week, and only have sex maybe once a month? Hell! What kind of choice was that? She'd accept sex with them both if it was only once ever! But more would definitely be better. Oh, yeah. She was gonna aim for more. Lots more.

* * * *

Boyd and Ryan snuggled together under their quilt. Although they each had their own rooms, with their own beds, closets, and desks, and they made sure to use their own rooms, they shared a bathroom that linked the two rooms, and they walked freely between them once their doors were bolted at night.

They also kept their cell phones with them at all times, and every person on the property had their cell numbers in case of an emergency.

But now, at night, alone together, snuggled under the quilt, they whispered their plans and hopes for the trip to the city next week.

"Do you think Vivi will join us? She's been very open and honest with us, but it's a big step to consider a threesome instead of something more traditional." Ryan pressed his lips to Boyd's shoulder and gently sucked the flesh there.

"I'm sure she'll give us a tryout. It's just up to us to blast her socks off so she wants to stay with us."

"Well, she did say the one night she'd had with two men was the best orgasm ever. But do you think she wants those men, instead of us?"

"Nah." Boyd shook his head assertively. "She's never even hinted at other men. Reckon it was a one-night stand or something like that. We know she was divorced a long time ago. It's not like a sexy chick like her would sleep alone the rest of her life. What we need to do is plan something really special, something memorable that will be the signal of the start of an ongoing relationship, not let her think we just want to use her for one night."

Boyd slid his fingers into Ryan's hair and pulled his face closer to kiss him deeply. Suddenly, the kiss got out of control. Noses mashed together, teeth clashed, and tongues slid between lips, cranking up the tension exponentially.

By the time they pulled apart, their lungs were starved for air, and their cocks were hot and hard with need.

"I can't wait any longer," whispered Boyd.

"Do me. Do me now." Ryan flung the quilt off them both and scrambled up to lean against the headboard, his legs spread wide apart and his hand on his cock.

Boyd rolled over and reached into the nightstand for the lube, wrenching the drawer open so hard it almost came off its tracks. He grabbed the lube, twisted the cap off, and was kneeling in front of Ryan in a heartbeat.

He squirted the lube into Ryan's anus then squeezed more gel over two fingers and slowly pressed them inside Ryan's hot, dark channel. Ryan pressed his ass back into Boyd's hand as the man's fingers massaged his inner walls. Both men's hips unconsciously rolled in time with the finger movements, and Ryan leaned forward and stroked Boyd's cock, capturing a pearly drop of cum from the eye and smoothing it over the mushroom-shaped cockhead.

"Fuck, that's hot," murmured Ryan.

"You're hotter. My dick is gonna burst if I don't get inside you soon."

"So hurry up and get inside."

"One more finger first." Boyd smeared lube liberally over his fingers again, entered Ryan's ass, and stretched the softened tissues gently before coating his cock in gel and dropping the tube onto the nightstand. "Now."

"Thank God. I thought you were gonna take all night!"

Boyd silenced him with another kiss while he pressed his engorged cock against Ryan's sphincter. The muscles opened easily, and he slid inside.

"Fuck, that feels good."

"Damn straight." Boyd pressed in farther, his cock sliding easily now, until he was balls-deep inside his lover.

They rested like that for a brief moment, arms wrapped around each other and lips locked together, then Boyd briskly withdrew almost all the way out until just his head remained inside Ryan, and he thrust deep and hard with all his power.

"Fuck, yes."

The men set up a punishing pace, Boyd pistoning in and out, muscles bunching and releasing, hips thrusting, sweat lightly coating his face and back. Ryan met him thrust for thrust, with harsh, needy strokes, one hand fisting his own cock, the other grasping Boyd, now on his shoulder, then on his hip, next on his upper arm.

The place was too frantic, the movements too harsh, for either of them to last long.

"I'm coming," gasped Boyd, swirling his hips in a figure eight, dragging his cock along all the sensitive nerves of Ryan's walls, and expertly pinging his prostate. Boyd took one hand off Ryan's hips to grip the other man's cock then thrust as hard and deep as he could.

His cock exploded in the hot, welcoming depths of his partner, and the jetting spurts of cum combined with all the other sensations to drive Ryan to climax, too. Cum spurted from Ryan's cock, coating both their hands and bellies.

Ryan leaned forward and pulled Boyd's face closer for another kiss. "We make a mighty fine team, you and me," he said.

"Hell, yeah. Give me ten minutes to recover, and let's do it again."

Laughing softly, they disentangled themselves and moved into the bathroom to clean up.

Chapter Seven

Vivi was quite nervous about meeting up with Boyd and Ryan again. The men were so hot, just looking at them made her thoughts scramble with the need to be fucked. But she wanted them to meet the young women in her care so the girls could ask questions about the project and what they would do there. On the other hand, if Boyd and Ryan were in her house, they couldn't have sex. And she really, really wanted to have sex with them. Well, as long as that's what they wanted, too.

She thought that's what they were leading to. They certainly seemed interested in her as a woman and said they shared a woman occasionally. They had even asked her if she'd ever slept with two men. But... *Ah, shit! What to do, what to say, what to plan.*

And that was without even considering the whole issue of their ages. She'd recently turned forty-one. She now knew Ryan was twenty-eight and Boyd twenty-nine, which meant there were twelve and thirteen years between them. She wasn't old enough to be their mother, but it was still a big gap. Life was so unfair. If she were the man and they the woman, no one would care about such a gap. But somehow, having the woman older was frowned upon.

So I guess that makes me a cougar. A double cougar. Maybe I should practice my growl. She giggled to herself.

"Go with the flow, Vivi. Just go with the flow." *Well, I don't have any other option, do I?* She sighed.

* * * *

The girls were a little shy around Boyd and Ryan at first. Both were big men, and some of the young women, Mikayla in particular, had good reason to be wary of large, charming men.

The ice was broken, though, when Neveah asked Boyd politely, "How do you like your coffee?" and he replied, "In a big mug."

Vivi gently steered the conversation into a discussion of the range of teas she'd brought back from her vacation, some of which the girls had really enjoyed after they'd gotten over the shock of seeing "leaves and sticks" in the teapot.

Ryan followed that with a description of the fruit juice shakes they made with their own fruit on the farm.

"You grow the fruit? Like, on trees and all?" asked a disbelieving Payton.

"Yes. We planted some of them as seedlings, so they won't have fruit for several years yet, but we also pruned and treated older trees already on the property, and they give us lots of fruit now. We make a fruit shake with apples and oranges, a little bit of grapefruit, and a few strawberries. Everyone likes them," added Boyd.

"Serious?" asked Genesis, her eyes wide.

"Absolutely," he replied.

The girls relaxed and peppered the men with questions about the lake, the ducks and chickens, and all the other projects.

"Are there horses?" asked Neveah suddenly.

"Yes, we have four horses, but they're work horses, not like the sleek, fast racehorses you see on TV. But if you want to learn to ride, Andy or Basil will teach you."

"Who's 'AndyorBasil'?"

"All the young people who come to the farm have to do an hour of reading and math each day. It's not like school." Ryan hurried on when he saw a few of the girls' faces falling. "It's useful things like working out how much rice you need for a recipe, how to read a bus timetable, how to know if someone is ripping you off on your utilities bill, how to plan where to stop overnight on a vacation trip, and how much you need to save each week to pay your cell phone bill."

Ryan looked around the table and saw the girls nodding and accepting what he'd said. He continued, "As well as that, if you want to go back to high school and graduate, we have makeup classes you can do." He saw Rylee nodding and remembered Vivi had said she hoped Rylee would go back to school.

"Yeah, but who's 'AndyorBasil'?" Genesis repeated.

"Andy, and Basil, are our two teachers. They live in the farm house with all the rest of us. Andy teaches most of the indoor subjects and Basil most of the outdoor ones, but they can each swap over a fair bit, too. And Boyd and I also help out, as well. While you are there, Vivienne will be with you, and she will teach some things, too. And Molly, our cook, will teach you cooking if there is anything you want to learn."

"Ya know, that small engine mechanics thing. Pulling stuff apart and fixin' it. I reckon I could do that. I hate school, and I'm never gonna be good at it. But I like tinkering with stuff. I once pulled a clock apart, and I got it back together, and it worked, too. Well, sorta worked," said Chloe.

Boyd smiled at her. "Basil will be happy to teach you. We do all our own maintenance on our equipment, and the boys have rebuilt a couple of old cars they use to drive around the farm. They're working on a pump to bring water from the dam to the orchard at the moment."

Chloe nodded. "I think I'd like doing that."

The conversation became general again, and Vivi was quite surprised when the doorbell rang and she noticed it was ten o'clock. She was even more surprised to find the couple who stayed with the girls on her days off standing there, a small bag in James' hand.

"James? Gina?"

"Since you'll be moving to the country for six months, we knew you'd have a ton of things to organize, hon."

"So we decided to come stay with the girls tonight and give you a head start."

"Off you go, and grab your purse, hon," added Gina, moving into the living room and hugging each girl in turn.

James gave Vivi a wink as he followed his wife inside.

Vivi turned to look at Boyd and Ryan, who were right behind her, ready to leave.

"Better get your purse like the lady said," echoed Ryan.

"You're a couple of smooth operators, now aren't you?" she muttered softly as she went to her room as instructed.

* * * *

Vivi was squeezed between the two men on the bench seat of their SUV as they drove into town.

"Where are we going?" she asked.

"We've booked a room in a hotel," replied Boyd, his deep, sexy voice sending chills and thrills right to her core.

"And?" she queried.

"It's a little bit different, but we think you'll like it," was all he added while Ryan quickly changed the topic of conversation.

They parked in a numbered space in the basement parking lot then were whisked up to the thirty-eighth floor in an elevator with mirrored walls and ceiling and a cool, green-tiled floor.

The hotel room was more like a suite, having a small sitting area with windows the length of the wall overlooking the city and a separate bedroom on the corridor side of the room with no external windows. Vivi was just thinking how unusual this was when the reason became apparent. The men led her to the bedroom doorway, switched on the light, and stood waiting for her comments.

The ceiling was painted a deep blue with stars, moons, and planets glowing and shimmering against the background.

One wall was a forest of tangled plants among tall trees with tiny flowers peeping out of the grass and ferns and creepers entwined around the tree trunks. As Vivi stood and stared at it, she saw birds hidden in the foliage, a monkey up one tree, and a rabbit peeping out from behind a clump of grass.

Slowly, she turned to the next wall. This was the wall in front of the bed, and it had more trees and grass leading to a waterfall, which fed into a deep pool. In the depths of the pool, she could see fish. A tiny frog perched on one of the rocks on the far side of the pool.

Vivi swiveled slowly and saw how cleverly the rocks at the far side of the pool blended into the third wall, which had the rocks leading to a sandy path and down to a beach. The sand was a pure, pristine gold with waves lapping the shore. Out on the horizon were a few boats with multicolored sails, and about halfway between the shore and the boats were a few dolphins playing with a mermaid.

Slowly, Vivi rotated a little farther, and the final wall was painted with trees and vines which seemed to surround and support the huge bed that backed into the wall. She noticed the painting blended seamlessly into the first wall she'd seen, the forest.

"What a simply amazing room. However did you find this place?"

"We contacted a company called Superior Vacations. They provide very special vacations, and when we said we wanted a room to impress a beautiful woman, they suggested this hotel. I can see you like it," said Boyd.

"Like it! It's way beyond 'like.' I've never seen anything so amazing, so stunningly beautiful. Someone must have spent forever imagining this then painting the murals. Wow! Just wow!" Vivi turned to Boyd and hugged him then repeated the gesture with Ryan.

"We wanted our first time together to be something to remember," said Ryan. "I know we haven't exactly discussed it, but we thought, we hoped…" He trailed off, looking at her with a worried frown between his eyes.

"Oh, yes. That's what I want, too. I want you both so much. But I need to tell you that the time I had sex with two men at once—that was with Superior Vacations. I..." Vivi stopped and drew in a big breath. "I wanted to try out a few different things sexually but wanted to do it in a controlled environment, so I used Superior Vacations."

Vivienne looked searchingly at them both, wondering if they would think her a slut.

But surprisingly, they both smiled. Ryan pulled her into his arms, and Boyd stepped up hard against her back, wrapping his arms around them both. "Oh, Vivi," he said in his deep bass voice. "The times we shared a woman—that was with Superior Vacations, too. I guess you could say that company has brought us all together."

Vivi relaxed with relief that her secret was out and had not disgusted them. "So now we can fuck?" she asked.

"No. Now we will make love," replied Ryan.

"Well, I suggest we all get naked then," Vivi said impishly.

With those few, simple words, sexual energy exploded in the room. All three of them had been lusting after each other for weeks now, and with the sharing of their lives, personalities, hopes, and dreams, had come a deep connection that demanded a sexual response.

Boyd inched closer to Vivi's back, and she could feel not only the hard wall of his chest pressed into her, but the equally hard ridge of his cock prodding the soft roundness of her ass.

In front of her, Ryan placed his hands on her hips and pressed his pelvis against hers. His cock was just as large and hard as Boyd's.

Instantly, Vivi's breath hitched, her heart pounded, and cream dripped onto her panties.

"God, you're both sexy," she whispered.

"We're about to show you just how very sexy we can be," murmured Ryan, gently pressing soft kisses along her jaw line. His lips moved to her forehead and whispered across it, tenderly kissing her temple, her eyebrows, her nose, and finally, her mouth.

Desire raged through Vivi. She gripped his head with both hands and ran her fingers through his long, dark hair. She'd wanted to do this since the moment she first saw him, and his hair was as soft and silky as she'd imagined it would be. Touching him served only to crank the heat inside her up another notch. Her fingers trailing through his hair and massaging his scalp, she ran her tongue along his lips then nibbled at his lower lip.

His cock jumped and grew even larger against her belly, and he thrust his tongue between her parted lips, using his long arms to haul Boyd hard against her, wrapping his arms around his partner and sandwiching Vivi between them so every muscle of Boyd's was pressed against her back and her butt, Boyd's cock was pushing against her ass, and her pelvis was wedged between hot, hard, hungry men. And she was on their menu.

Yum!

Boyd's lips traced along her neck, sending erotic shivers up and down her spine, and Vivi wiggled with excitement. Her panties were soaked, need was burning in her veins, and tension coiled in her belly, demanding action.

Without giving her any warning, the two men picked her up, still wedged between them, and carried her over to the bed. There, she was settled on the deep blue blanket, and four hands were suddenly undressing her. In the shortest possible space of time, her jeans, shirt, sandals, and underwear disappeared, and Ryan was pulling off his shirt while Boyd toed off his own shoes.

Vivi rested back on an elbow and watched as the men shucked their clothing at lightning speed, leaving it in a tangled heap on the floor, which a distant part of her brain registered was a pretty, moss-green tile.

Her mind registered broad shoulders, muscled arms, backs and chests, long, strong bodies, narrow hips, muscular legs. *God, they look good. And they are mine. Well, at least for tonight, they're mine.*

Then she was once again sandwiched between the men, and her brain ceased to function at all.

Four hands stroked and caressed her ribs, her breasts, her arms, and her hips. Two mouths dropped kisses on her face and her breasts. Several legs tangled with hers. Silky black hair pressed against her chest, making her nipples tingle.

Desperately, Vivi stretched out her own hands to touch and pressed her own lips to the nearest pieces of naked skin to lick and taste. Her cunt was dripping cream, quivering and clenching with the need to be filled. Her nipples were as hard as diamonds, pressing into the male chests leaning over her, demanding more stroking, demanding to be pinched or sucked or something, anything.

"Enough foreplay. Just fuck me," she begged.

Both men reached for the nightstand simultaneously, almost tipping the three of them off the bed because their bodies were so intertwined.

Vivi grabbed the nearest arm and held on as Ryan opened the drawer and Boyd reached for a couple of condoms and a tube of lube.

"There's a lot of good stuff in here. We'll have to try it out. Later," Boyd rasped, his voice hoarse with passion, as he rolled them all back into the middle of the bed.

The three disentangled themselves a bit, then Boyd pushed Vivi onto her back while Ryan kneeled up and held her legs up and wide apart so Boyd could start lubing her ass. The two men worked very slowly and thoroughly, massaging the sphincter muscle until Boyd's fingers slid easily inside her. Then he painstakingly smoothed the cool gel all around her walls, stretching and loosening the tissues, scissoring his fingers to make her opening wider and ready for a cock.

Vivi stared at their cocks. Both were long and wide, but Boyd's was definitely wider, the head broader and now a deep red with need.

Ryan's cock was wide, too, but not as broad as Boyd's, and the head was sleeker, more streamlined. His cock was a little longer than Boyd's, though, and it was almost purplish with intense arousal.

With her body braced on her elbows to watch them and her legs in the air, Vivi couldn't touch either of the men, but just looking at them, feeling their hands on her, was enough to keep her at an incredibly high level of arousal.

Finally, they were satisfied she was prepared for them, and Boyd dropped the lube back on the nightstand, grabbing a scented wipe to cleanse his fingers before passing a condom to Ryan and rolling his own condom on. Then Vivi watched Ryan roll a rubber down his cock and squeeze lube on it.

Tingles were racing up and down Vivienne's spine. Her whole body was one giant erogenous zone trembling with desire to be filled. Just seeing these two men naked was almost enough to bring her to climax. She wanted to be possessed, filled, fucked so bad, but she was half afraid she'd orgasm the moment they touched her, she was so aroused just from being with them.

Boyd and Ryan surrounded her, closing their arms around her, each one kissing her sweetly on the lips, first Ryan, then Boyd.

"Are you ready? Do you want this?" asked Boyd, his deep bass voice rumbling through her body, making every nerve-ending scream with sexual tension.

"Both of us inside you together?" clarified Ryan.

The men looked deep into her eyes, and Vivi nodded, fully understanding that they were trying to be completely fair to her.

"Yes, that's what I want. I want you both inside me, both of you together. And I want you to do it now, dammit. I'm tired of waiting here!" she replied.

As if she'd thrown a switch, both men moved fast. Boyd grabbed her legs and pulled her right into the center of the big bed then slid on top of her, pushing her legs wide with his hips as he slithered down her body.

His fingers teased her clit for a few moments then slid into the warm, clutching heat of her cunt. "Oh, yes, you're ready," he said as he withdrew them and held his penis to the opening of her channel. He pressed deep inside.

Vivi sighed with joy. He was very broad and stretched her to the limit. But she felt so wonderfully, joyfully filled. God, it was good to have a man inside her once again. Especially this man, these men, whom she'd been lusting after for so long.

Boyd hooked his legs around her body and rolled them over so he was on his back and she was on top of him.

Remembering her experience with Caleb and David, Vivi flattened her body against his chest and tilted her ass into the air.

"That's right," soothed Ryan as he pulled her ass cheeks apart and dripped some more lube inside her before pressing his sheathed cock at the entry to her dark channel.

Very, very slowly, a fraction of an inch at a time, Ryan pressed his cock inside her. It soon popped through the ring of muscles and slid easily and deeply into her. Because Boyd was already filling her pussy, Ryan's penis in her ass was a tight fit, stretching her tissues and making her feel unbelievably full. But it was a good feeling, too. A slight burn, but mostly a feeling of intense possession. She felt claimed, adored, possessed, and was clutched so tightly between the two men, her every breath seemed to be a part of them. She could feel their hearts beating on either side of her, feel their breaths tickling her body, feel their cocks twitch inside her, and never had anything felt this good before.

"Ready, sweetheart?" asked Ryan.

"Yes," breathed Vivi.

Ryan took his weight on his forearms and lifted off her, gradually withdrawing his cock until only the head was left inside her. Then, as he pushed back in again, Boyd gradually pulled out. Their cocks rubbed each other against the thin membrane separating her channels, and Vivi shivered in ecstasy.

When Ryan was fully inside her again and just the head of Boyd's cock remained inside, the men reversed the process, moving in tiny increments at a time, drawing the process out in a slow, steady glide.

Vivi lifted her breasts to press her incredibly sensitive, aching nipples into Boyd's chest.

She wrapped her arms backward to grab around Ryan's waist and held him to her. When they were both midway in the maneuver, she swirled her hips in a quick figure eight, feeling both cocks scrape against her walls. It felt so delicious she did it again and again.

Ryan hissed through his teeth, and Boyd grabbed hold of Ryan to unite the three of them together once more. "Fuck, you'll get me off, and this will be over before it's hardly begun."

Carefully, the men pulled Vivi into a sitting-up posture, their legs all tangled together and their three torsos pressed firmly into each other. The men wrapped their arms around each other so Vivi could hardly move, but they let her put her arms up so they were all three holding hands together, fingers as entwined as their legs.

Now the two men moved together, pulling out together, pushing in together. Vivi was so stretched and full, so pressed between them she could hardly breathe, but her body was alive with sensation, and need coiled like a spring deep in her core.

She could feel every twitch of their cocks, every little movement of their muscles, even Boyd's eyelashes as he pressed his face into her neck. She had never felt so cherished before in her life, so adored and loved.

Deep inside her, an orgasm was gathering. It boiled up through her limbs, firing along her nerves, building in her breasts and pussy and ass. But it was also exploding in her heart, as she knew for an absolute fact that she loved these men, both of them, and that she wanted a relationship with them for as long as they wanted her.

The realization slammed through her mind just as both men thrust deep and hard into her body. Vivi threw back her head and screamed as an intensely powerful climax roared through every part of her and erupted, shaking her until she thought she would have broken into a million pieces if Ryan and Boyd hadn't been holding her so tightly.

She felt hot cum jetting into the condoms in her cunt and her ass as both men climaxed with her. The cocks kept moving in her as aftershocks rolled through them all, her orgasm going on and on as her body shook with its power.

Chapter Eight

Vivi sagged limply in their arms as the orgasm gradually slowed down. Their fingers loosed from hers as they let her relax. Ryan pulled out first and left the room.

Oh, yeah. This room has murals everywhere. The bathroom must be off the living room of the suite.

She was cuddled into Boyd, almost asleep, when Ryan returned and pulled her back into his arms, allowing Boyd to leave.

She was dozing when she felt herself swept off the bed and carried out of the bedroom. She realized some time must have passed when they reached the bathroom, as a giant hot tub had been filled with water and the scent of lavender was in the air.

The room was not quite as spectacular as the bedroom but was still very nice, with glass walls and sparkling white fittings everywhere.

Ryan handed her into the hot tub into Boyd's arms then rummaged through the bathroom cabinet for some lavender lotion and shower gel.

She sank into the hot water and leaned back against Ryan. "Mmmm, nice," she murmured.

The men looked at each other over her head. "Are you ready to talk about the future?" asked Boyd.

"Yeah, sure. I thought we'd pretty much settled what I would be doing on the farm when the girls and I arrive for our six months there. And the charity is happy for any of them to stay on longer if they want to go back to high school or complete a training course with you."

"What Boyd means is not talk about *the* future, but talk about *our* future," clarified Ryan.

"I sort of guessed having sex on the farm might be a big no-no," said Vivi, turning in Ryan's arms to watch their faces carefully.

"Not exactly. Just as you do, we're supposed to be modeling real life, but a way of life that is socially responsible and that contributes to the community. Boyd and I each have our own rooms, but we share a connecting bathroom, and at night we move back and forth between the rooms. Most of the young adults know we are together, but we don't flaunt the relationship."

Vivi nodded. She understood what Ryan was saying, but her heart was pounding so hard it was difficult to think straight. She was sure they wanted her. They'd gone to so much trouble to make this good for her. But she couldn't see where the conversation was leading, couldn't guess what they would say next.

Boyd grabbed the bottle of shower gel and smeared a generous dollop on the tile wall behind the hot tub. With one finger, he drew an outline of the front of the farm house.

"This is the girls' wing, this is the boys' wing, and here are our rooms. We plan to build an extra room on at the front here, like a sunroom, with a big wall of glass out to the east. Plant a bunch of flowering shrubs to look pretty."

Vivi just nodded. It all sounded great, but she was confused. What the hell was his point?

"The sunroom will be our private living room. Behind it will be an extra bedroom—yours."

"So each of our three rooms will have a separate entry from the corridor, but we can move from one to the other internally through the new sunroom. Plus it will give us some private space, our own retreat," added Ryan.

"And we can do a lot of the work ourselves, so it won't be too expensive. Several of the young men want to learn carpentry, so working under a trained builder will be excellent experience for them.

Even the glazing they may be able to help with. And certainly the interior fitting-out."

"But what happens in six months' time when I leave?" asked Vivi.

"Ahh, yeah, well, umm…" Ryan looked at Boyd, then the two of them drew Vivi into their arms.

"We were hoping you wouldn't leave. If you stay, we can expand the program for young women—"

Ryan's sentence was cut off with a splash as Boyd pushed him under the water. "Dumbass! You're supposed to say we both love her first, then talk about the program!"

Ryan rubbed his hands over his face and shook water out of his ears. "But you know we love you, don't you? Don't you?"

Vivi could only laugh at the stunned look on his face. "I hoped. I guessed. But it's nice to hear the words, as well. I've only just realized how very much I love you both."

Dramatically, both men kneeled in the water, and each took one of her hands in his. "I, Ryan—"

"And I, Boyd—"

"—love you, Vivi. And I—"

"—*We* want you to move in with us."

"Yes, we do."

Vivi reached forward and drew them both into her arms. "I accept," she said simply.

THE END

http://berengariasblog.blogspot.com/

Siren Publishing

Ménage Amour

Tenealle

Berengaria Brown

TEMPTING TENEALLE

BERENGARIA BROWN
Copyright © 2011

Chapter One

Tenealle sighed as she carefully stepped over all the sleeping bodies on her great room floor. It was 6:55 a.m., and she needed to be online at her day job at seven a.m.

Shaking her head as she circumnavigated Cousin Mark, who seemed even larger in his sleeping bag than his awake six-foot, two-hundred-pound self, Tenealle squeezed past a pile of luggage and into her tiny office.

"Thank God," she whispered as she booted up her computer. *Why, oh why, did Dad have to be the youngest of ten children? If he'd had the good sense to be an only child like Mom, I wouldn't have a bazillion cousins invading my great room!*

Tenealle clicked into her company chat room and was soon busily making notes about her day's tasks. One of the managers was off-loading some of his clients onto her manager, who had responded by dumping his in-tray into Tenealle's inbox.

The extra money I make from this new work will be great, but first I need to get rid of all these cousins before they eat everything in my kitchen! And I really need a bigger apartment. I just know there'll be a riot if they all want to use my little bathroom at once.

Silence reigned for several hours, though, and Tenealle made the most of it, answering e-mails, filling in spreadsheets, and rearranging her workload to incorporate the most urgent of the new tasks.

By the time her tummy was rumbling with the need for breakfast, there were noises coming from the great room, indicating that at least some of her cousins were awake.

Tenealle stretched. *Half past nine. No wonder I'm hungry. I'd better put on some coffee and toast for them.*

After carefully logging off from all her work files, Tenealle opened her office door. One sleeping body was still stretched out on her floor, but chatter from her kitchen indicated at least some of her unwanted guests were getting their own meals.

"Jeez, Tenealle. Don't you ever shop?" asked Drew. "There are only two eggs here and no sausages, no bacon, and no hash browns. What are we supposed to eat?"

"Muesli. That's what I have. And there's bread if you want toast."

"Not even a full loaf. That works out at maybe two slices each, if we're lucky."

"Empower yourself, Drew. Go down to the store, buy what you want, and then cook it yourself," suggested Tenealle.

"Like that's gonna happen," joked Mark. "The only reason we're staying in this sardine can you call an apartment is because we're all broke."

"Well, apart from the fact we all love you, of course," added Drew wisely.

"Uh-huh," replied Tenealle, pulling the almost empty box of muesli from the cupboard. "I see you found my muesli."

"Pretty sure that was Jack. He got the munchies around midnight."

"When are you all leaving?" she asked sternly but couldn't keep the grin off her face or out of her voice. Her cousins were total pains in the ass, but she loved them anyway.

Tim stepped into the kitchen wearing nothing but a towel. "There's no hot water left, guys. Looks like I won't be shaving this morning."

"I really, really need a bigger apartment," sighed Tenealle.

"And more food, and more hot water," added Tim, grabbing the last tomato out of the refrigerator. "Don't you ever buy food?" he continued, unconsciously echoing Drew.

Tenealle snatched the milk carton out of Mark's hand and poured the last of the milk over her muesli. "There's fifty dollars in the coffee jar. Buy food. Buy milk. Buy bread. But make sure there is something here for me to eat for lunch. I have a heap of work to do, and I can't keep a roof over all of our heads unless I'm fed!"

"Don't worry, Cuz. We'll shop this morning. Then we're going to visit Great-Uncle Albert this afternoon. And tonight is Jack's game. We'll all be out of your way by noon tomorrow."

The talk became general then, mostly about Jack's Scrabble tournament. Jack would be at the conference center watching the other players all day. His match was at four p.m. The quarterfinals were played simultaneously at six p.m., the semifinals at seven, then the grand final at eight thirty, with the medal presentations around ten p.m.

Jack was a very good player, but only ranked twenty-fifth, so even though Tenealle was confident he'd make it at least to the quarterfinals, they would all be there to support him for his match at four. Meanwhile, she had a mountain of work to deal with. Tenealle put her bowl and spoon in the sink and headed back into her office.

* * * *

Jack thrilled them all by getting as far as the semifinals and scoring a personal best before being eliminated. They all went to Dumpling King to celebrate after the medal presentations, arriving back at Tenealle's apartment in the early hours of the morning.

By the time her cousins finally departed at midday the next day, Tenealle's kitchen looked like a bomb had hit it, and her refrigerator and food cupboard bore a close resemblance to Old Mother Hubbard's cupboard. Empty. And of course there was no hot water left. As she waved them good-bye, Tenealle held on to her sanity by chanting in her head, *Must move to a bigger apartment. Must move to a bigger apartment. Must move to a bigger apartment...*

Tenealle concentrated on her most urgent work projects. Then, after a meal of rice, which was pretty much the only edible thing left in her kitchen, she settled in front of her computer again to look at vacant apartments.

I need space. I need at least one guest room. I must have a second bathroom. And it would be really good if my office was separated from the living area. Likely, that will be impossible at the price I can afford.

Sipping on a cup of hot coffee—black because the cousins had drunk the milk they'd bought—Tenealle looked at apartment after apartment. Anything even vaguely promising was out of her price range.

Maybe a fixer-upper, she thought, clicking on another Web site. And there it was. An "office with dwelling" in a warehouse district. It was a top-floor apartment from a deceased's estate, and the heir did not want it. There was a small reception foyer and an office with a bathroom, then a hallway through to a two-bedroom apartment with a full bathroom and large living area. Between the front office and the rear apartment was a private courtyard garden. The whole was listed as "in need of love and attention but structurally sound," and the price was within her means.

It was much too late to call the agent now, but Tenealle bookmarked the site to call the agent at nine tomorrow. Then she returned to her kitchen to restore it to some semblance of order and write a shopping list. "Preferably before I starve," she reminded herself as she stared into the empty refrigerator.

* * * *

Faris Barker sat on the stone edge of the fountain, smiling as his partner, Evan Schmidt, prowled up and down the courtyard garden, kicking at the occasional weed that had poked its head up between the flagstones, and slapping at the overgrown shrubs and trees as he walked past.

"Relax, man. This place just needs a gardener. There's nothing much wrong with it, really." He kicked his heels against the stone base of the fountain. "Solid as a rock. Quite literally."

Evan grinned back. "A gardener, right? And a painter for the rooms, a handyman to make the doors shut properly, a dude to resurface the floors—"

"Yeah, but those are details. Incidentals. There's nothing wrong with the building. No wood rot, or insects, or black mold, or anything. This woman will love it and buy it, and you can go back to your lair and forget all about your great-aunt Enid."

"I can remember when she was well, and this garden was so beautiful. It looks sad now, but she always had pretty flowers in bloom, all year round, and there were fish in that fountain."

"Fish? In the fountain?"

"Yeah, she always was an independent-minded woman."

"Fish. You know, I like that idea. And we could get someone to prune and weed and plant flowers."

"Uh-huh. Not to mention paint the walls, sand the floorboards, replace all the floor coverings, fix the other stuff. Can you imagine the mess? The stink of paint and varnish? No way. Much better to sell it and forget it," said Evan.

Faris looked at his cell phone. "Ah well, the woman will be here in five minutes and will likely be the answer to all your prayers."

"Not all my prayers, surely. She may buy the apartment and get that off my hands, but she's not likely to be a glorious redhead, with a lush body, who just happens to want to fuck two men at once."

"No. One step at a time, I guess. Although I like the name Tenealle, and she sounded about our age on the phone. She had a pleasant, friendly voice, so you never know."

The door buzzer interrupted them.

Evan hurried back into the living room of the apartment, then up the hallway, to answer the door. The garden could only be accessed from the house, not from the office, making it more private—something Faris decided he really liked—but a longer walk to the front door. In fact, Faris liked the whole apartment and could visualize its potential to be the perfect place for them both, once it had been upgraded a little. *Too bad Evan doesn't agree.* He stood to his feet and followed his partner inside.

By the time Faris reached the office, Evan had opened the door and was standing, dumbstruck, in front of the most gorgeous woman Faris had ever seen. She was tall for a woman, about five-eight, with a lush, curvaceous body, huggable hips, suckable breasts, and sparkling chocolate eyes. And, holy hell! Red hair. Goddamn it, she was everything Evan had asked for, and more, wrapped up in the most enticing package Faris had ever seen.

His cock woke, stretched, and damn near burst out of his pants at his first sight of her. He was hard enough to pound nails, ready to push her up against the nearest wall and fuck her, and he hadn't even spoken a single word to her yet! Where the hell had that come from?

Noticing that Evan seemed totally incapable of social niceties due to shock, he punched the other man on the arm, then held out his hand. "I'm Faris Barker, Evan Schmidt's partner. I'm guessing you're Tenealle Jones. Great to meet you, Ms. Jones."

"Please call me Tenealle. I see what you mean by 'needs some care,' but I like the proportions of this room."

Evan still seemed to be totally gobsmacked, so Faris explained. "Evan's great-aunt Enid has lived here for a very long time. Originally she and her husband ran an accounting business out of these few rooms and lived in the rear apartment. There's a small bathroom through here."

Faris opened the door, and Tenealle walked through. He tried to see the room through Tenealle's eyes. It had a toilet, shower, and sink and hadn't been used much for some years. The ceramic ware was a little stained, but it might scrub up okay. Or maybe she'd want to replace it with a dual-flush model. If it was up to him, he'd retile the room in sunny yellow and cool blues.

Evan had pulled himself together now and began describing the apartment's amenities—security, privacy, a well-run building in a reasonable neighborhood. Then he showed Tenealle the smaller internal office. She pulled out a notepad and sketched the rooms, marking in electrical outlets and built-in cupboards.

"What about Internet access?" Tenealle asked.

"No worries there. Great-Aunt Enid was quite computer savvy, and she had cable TV. Whatever you want should be good."

The scrumptious redhead paced around the two rooms and made some more notes, then followed Evan down the hallway to the living area of the apartment.

"Both these doors have secure locks on them, so no one can get into the apartment without keys while you're in the office," pointed out Evan as he opened the apartment door, then waved back toward the door from the office area.

"This hallway runs the length of the interior courtyard and garden, which is only accessible from the apartment."

"The office has no external windows for security's sake," added Faris, "but there's lots of natural light in the apartment."

"I like that it's secure, but I'm not a wimp. I've been living on my own for ten years now," said Tenealle. Then she muttered something that sounded like, "Apart from when a bazillion cousins descend on me."

A bazillion cousins? What the hell? Could a person, especially someone as delicious as Tenealle Jones, even have a bazillion cousins? How many was a bazillion anyway? *I must have misheard her.*

Evan walked Tenealle through the apartment's two bedrooms, the large bathroom between them, a comfortable kitchen with dining area, and the spacious living room opening out into the garden courtyard.

Tenealle wrote page after page of notes in her little notebook, paced out room sizes, checked for cupboards and electrical outlets—what was her hang-up with them?—then strolled around the garden.

Faris trailed behind them, noticing the way her delicious ass flexed as she moved, how her lush hips swayed, and the way she smiled at him and Evan whenever they caught her gaze. She smiled with her whole face, not just her eyes, and it lit up with pleasure and happiness.

Damn, but she's hot. Hotter than hot. Hotter than hell. Oh, how I'd love to get inside her pants. I wonder if she's wearing panties? There's no visible panty line, and those jeans are welded to her skin in all the right places. Damn. Gotta get my mind off her ass before my dick breaks my zipper.

Faris and Evan enjoyed sharing a woman. They were both bisexual, both committed to each other, and both looking for a woman to complete their relationship. But while women who wanted to try two men at once were easy enough to find, women who wanted a permanent ménage relationship were a lot scarcer. And so far none of the available ones had appealed to them both. Could Tenealle really be the one they were searching for? She certainly pressed every one of his buttons. She was a wet dream come to life. And from the stunned look on Evan's face when Faris had walked into the office, plus the stiff-legged way Evan had been moving through the house ever since she'd arrived, his partner's mind was running along much the same track as his own. But how was he supposed to find out if she liked them both? Somehow he knew "Wanna fuck two men at once?" was likely not going to be a successful pickup line.

Faris's gaze followed Tenealle as she walked gracefully around the garden. She stood still on the far side of the fountain, pulled out her cell phone, and made—or maybe answered—a call.

Then she returned to the living room, her chocolate eyes sparkling. Turning to Evan she said, "Knock ten thousand dollars off the price, and I'll take it today."

"What?"

"Reduce the price by ten thousand, and I'll sign the sale note now."

"But—But—"

Faris couldn't help himself. He burst out laughing. One minute Evan couldn't wait to sell the property. The next minute he received an offer and didn't know what to do.

Tenealle stared at them. Then her face grew hard. "Is this some kind of a joke? Is this apartment for sale or not? Give me a straight yes-or-no answer right now."

Faris sobered up and looked at Evan.

Evan managed to pull himself together. "Yes, it is for sale. How about I take five thousand dollars off the price and we meet at my attorney's tomorrow to sign the paperwork?"

"What time tomorrow?"

"Let me get it organized." Evan made a call, then said to Tenealle, "Either at ten thirty or at three thirty. He can fit us in at either of those times."

Tenealle pulled her cell phone out again and pressed her speed dial. "Hey Herb, how does ten thirty tomorrow suit you? Oh, okay, the other option is three thirty. Ten thirty's better? Okay, I'll e-mail you the address when I get home. See you there. Bye."

"Ten thirty it is. Where is your attorney's office?" she asked.

Evan told her the details, then asked, "Tenealle…um…tomorrow…um, after the paperwork is done, would you and your attorney join Faris, me, and my attorney for lunch? Just a little celebration?"

"Isn't that kind of unusual?"

"Likely it is. But I'd—we'd—like to get to know you a little more. Unless, that is…Should we be inviting your significant other as well?"

"Oh no, no significant other, but about a thousand cousins. Herbert is the only cousin I'll welcome to lunch, though."

"Only a thousand cousins? I thought you had a bazillion?"

"Oh, I do, I do. I trip over them wherever I go. My father was the youngest of ten children, and the city is littered with my cousins. In fact, just about every major city in America is home to at least one of them! They're everywhere! So, may I take some photographs of the rooms so I can start planning paint colors and where my furniture will fit?"

"Of course. Let me walk around with you," agreed Evan.

"Me too," added Faris.

* * * *

"So how are we going to get her into our bed with two attorneys also at the dinner table?" asked Evan.

"Damned if I know. But I reckon we use the meal to make another date with her, with seduction as the game plan."

"Uh-huh. What do you suggest? Wine, dine, and dance? A movie?"

"How about a day out somewhere innocuous? Somewhere she couldn't possibly refuse to go. Like the zoo or an art gallery," suggested Faris.

"Oh, I like that idea. Let's give her the choice. The zoo or the Beecher Gallery. If she's in control of choosing the venue, she'll likely feel happier about coming out with us, and more relaxed about accepting a date. Damn, I couldn't believe it when I opened the door and there was this red-hot redhead standing there. I thought I was dreaming."

"Yeah, me too. But her hair isn't really red. It's kind of a brownish-red."

"Who cares what color her hair is? She's damn hot. Her breasts. Her hips. And did you notice the way her whole face lights up when she smiles? It's not just her mouth, or even her eyes and her mouth. It's everything. Like the sunshine coming out after the rain. It's just so beautiful. *She's* incredibly beautiful."

"I did notice. And she is beautiful, an absolute wet dream come to life. But in the meantime, you and I are here together, and there is a nice bed just waiting for us to climb into it."

"I do like the way you think."

Faris pulled Evan into his arms, and they just held each other for a long moment. Then they both moved forward to grind their pelvises together, their cocks rubbing each other through the layers of clothing.

Faris wrapped his arms tightly around Evan and pressed his lips to his partner. He was just a few inches taller than the other man and had to dip his head a fraction to achieve a perfect meshing of their mouths.

Evan's tongue licked along the seam of Faris's lips, and he opened immediately, welcoming the other man in.

Suddenly the sexual tension blossomed at an extreme level, and their tongues began thrusting wildly, their hips pressing together, and their arms pulling their bodies as close to each other as possible.

"Bed," gasped Faris.

They quickly moved into their bedroom, and Evan unbuttoned Faris's shirt, while Faris undid Evan's belt and pulled down his zipper. He loved the feel of Evan's cock in his hands. It was so hot, so thick, so silky soft, and yet so hard. But above all, it felt so damn good inside him. He loved to fuck, but he also loved being fucked. Both were distinctly different pleasures, but with Evan, both were so very, very good.

Faris gently stroked Evan's cock, running a fingernail along the vein, then under the head, where he knew Evan was very sensitive.

Evan's gasp was an adequate reward for his efforts, Then Evan's hands pushed his shirt open, and his fingers were tweaking Faris's nipples. The flat little nubs were doing their very best to stand up and be noticed.

"Bed. Now," Faris ordered.

Quickly they shucked the rest of their clothes and climbed into their bed. Faris kneeled on all fours, letting Evan know he wanted to be bottom this time.

Evan slapped Faris's ass. "God, I love you like that. You have a great ass, and it's all mine."

Evan got their lube from the nightstand and squirted a little into Faris's ass. Then he inserted a slippery finger deep inside. He carefully stretched and massaged Faris's walls, adding more gel and a second finger after a few minutes.

Faris was eagerly pressing back into Evan's fingers, and using one hand, he stroked his own cock, which was almost painfully hard. "Now. Fuck me now."

There was the sound of latex snapping, and then Evan's hands were on Faris's hips, and Evan's cock was pushing its way into Faris's eagerly waiting butt.

As Evan's cock popped through the ring of muscle, Faris sighed. "Oh yeah. That's what I needed. You feel so very good."

"I love being inside you. You're so hot, so welcoming. But I've gotta move. I can't hold on long."

"So move already." And with that, Faris pushed back hard, impaling himself on Evan's cock.

After a few jerky thrusts, the two of them got a good rhythm going, of thrust and retreat, in and out, the slap of Evan's balls against the back of Faris's thighs underlining the men's grunts and gasps.

Faris was burning to come. His cock was about to explode, and he knew if he so much as touched himself, it would. Evan's hands were gripping his hips as he powered in and out, and Faris pushed back desperately into the strokes.

Evan let go with one hand and reached around to grab Faris's cock. He stroked firmly from root to balls, then swiveled his hips so his cock rubbed the walls of Faris's hot, dark channel. With a deep groan, Faris exploded, his cum spurting powerfully from his penis, up onto his belly.

Evan thrust once more, twice, then jetted his cum into Faris's butt, the heat of his seed burning hot even through the thin rubber protection.

After a few more strokes, Evan, still buried in Faris, rolled them to their sides so they lay sweating, panting, yet still connected together.

"That was very good. We really must do it again sometime," joked Faris.

"Oh, we will, we will. Just give me ten minutes to get my breath back," replied Evan.

Chapter Two

Tenealle was nervously pacing up and down outside the attorney's office when Cousin Herbert pulled up in his shiny new SUV. She waved at her small, beat-up, bright red compact car and grinned at him. "Business going well, is it, Herb?"

"Yeah, but it's more that Emma is almost through college now, and I get to spend my money on myself instead of on her," he joked.

Titus, Joab, and Co. was a smartly furnished historical building with a lot of gray—gray paint on the walls, gray stone counter, plush gray rugs underfoot.

"Soothing, I suppose," Tenealle whispered.

Mr. Titus himself opened the door to welcome them into his office. Tenealle's breath hitched at the gorgeous picture Evan and Faris made, standing together by the window. *Shit, they're hot. Sex on a stick times two.*

Faris had to be at least six foot two, a long, lean drink of water with shaggy blond hair and deep blue eyes. Evan was likely an even six foot, with dark brown hair touching the collar of his button-down shirt, a shirt that was straining at all the seams to accommodate his muscular chest and upper arms.

And I bet his thighs are just as ripped. Oh man, look at that cock!

"Tenealle? *Tenealle!*"

She snapped out of her daze and looked at Herb, who nodded slightly toward Mr. Titus, who was waiting to shake her hand.

"Adam Titus, my dear. Herbert Jones is known to me by reputation, of course. I believe you are related to him?"

"He's my cousin. One of my many cousins."

"Ah, yes. Herbert does seem to have a lot of cousins."

"Oh, we do, we do. His father was son number two. My father was kid number ten."

"Seventy-two cousins and counting," added Herb helpfully.

"Seventy-two!" echoed Faris.

"Told you there were bazillions of them. But that counts second and third cousins and so on," Tenealle explained.

"Shall we begin?" interrupted Adam Titus.

Tenealle pretty much just sat and listened. Everything sounded fine to her, but she was no expert. That's why Herb was there.

Light blue paint for the office would be nice. Maybe with one deeper blue feature wall. And purplish-blue tiles for the entryway and office floor to be easily cleaned. Now, I think Cousin Bruce did carpentry. I must ask Tim. He'll know. And I'm sure Mark's sister, Jodie, was studying agriculture, or horticulture, or landscaping, or something. I bet she could advise me about the garden. It could be so beautiful, I know it...

"So we're all agreed, then?" Titus's voice penetrated her thoughts. She nodded along with the others, signed where she was told to sign, and handed over a bank check for more than half her savings.

"Although it's a thirty-day settlement, Mr. Schmidt is happy to let you have a key straightaway so you can begin work on the property if that is your desire," Mr. Titus said.

"That would be wonderful. I want to talk to various tradespeople about things I need to get done, and they'll want to see the apartment, I expect. I've got some ideas about what I want already."

"Good, good. I believe a table is waiting for us for an early lunch at Sally's. Shall we continue the conversation there?" suggested Mr. Titus.

They all traveled to the restaurant in Herb's SUV to simplify the car parking. Tenealle welcomed the arrangement. She was fascinated with Faris and Evan and happy to share the backseat with them while Adam Titus and Herb discussed lawyer-type stuff up front.

"What do you do, Tenealle? Why do you need an office?" asked Evan.

"I have an office in my current apartment, but it's the second bedroom, and I seem to suffer a constant stream of visiting cousins who then have to sleep on the floor of my great room. They use all my hot water and eat me out of house and home."

"Yes, I see why you need a bigger apartment, but you didn't actually answer the question," said Faris.

"Oh, sorry. I'm a scheduler. I schedule relief carers for families with a child with disabilities, or for someone caring for an ill or elderly family member. The company has a team of part-time personal care attendants, and I keep spreadsheets of who's available when, who has cared for whom in the past, and make the bookings when a carer is ill, or tired, or just needs a break. Likely that sounds really boring, but I enjoy the challenges of fitting the pieces together like jigsaw puzzles."

"Yeah, I can see it would be really hard when the Super Bowl is on or the flu is going around or something," said Evan.

"Exactly. How about you two? Do you work together or what?"

"We work for the same company—" began Evan.

"But in different departments," added Faris. "I'm an accountant, and he's an IT nerd."

Tenealle asked a few questions about their work, and by the time they arrived at Sally's, they were happily chatting like old friends.

The lunch went very smoothly, with everyone getting along well together, and it seemed like no time at all to Tenealle when Herbert looked at his watch and jumped up.

"Hell! I'm going to be late for my next appointment if we don't leave right now. Sorry, to break up the party, folks, but I've gotta rush."

"Not a problem, I need to leave about now, too," said Adam Titus.

"We've got the day off, so we'll stay a bit longer and catch a cab back to your office later, Adam, if that's okay?" said Faris.

Tenealle was torn. She was enjoying talking to these gorgeous hunks, but she did not, officially at least, have the day off and really ought to get back to her computer.

"Stay a little longer," begged Evan. "Surely you don't have to leave just yet."

"I have a stack of things I should be doing." She hesitated. *Damn it, I'll stay.*

"It's okay, Herb, Mr. Titus. I'll stay on a little longer and catch a taxi back with Evan and Faris."

Evan ordered more coffee, and Faris followed that up by ordering a cheese platter, so Tenealle relaxed back in her chair, prepared to stay up until midnight, if necessary, to clear her in-tray when she finally got home.

The conversation took off again as they talked about everything and nothing: politics, movies, singers, the weather. Their discussions ranged all over the spectrum, and Tenealle found herself enjoying their company as she hadn't enjoyed anyone's, not even the nicest cousins', for a long time.

And, God, they were hot. Tenealle was sure every female in Sally's Restaurant was envying her, sitting there with not one, but two of the best-looking men in town. Men who laughed and smiled, who joked and offered serious opinions, men who made her feel beautiful and special, even though she hardly knew them.

And oh, how she wanted to know them more. They seemed to be so genuinely nice, as well as intelligent and quick-thinking, and incredibly easy on the eyes. Evan had muscles everywhere. The man was totally ripped. And Faris was the perfect contrast, long and lean with a runner's build. *Hmm, I'd love to lick and touch every inch of both of them. Such a shame it won't happen.* She sighed. Just looking at them made her so hot. She was creaming with desire for both of them. Her panties were damp, and her belly was clenching, and she'd never even kissed either of them! If they so much as touched her, she was sure she'd come on the spot. She was absolutely certain she would. *How the hell did that happen? I only met them yesterday. It's not like I really even know them. And there's two of them!*

"Which do you prefer, Tenealle? The zoo or the art museum?" asked Faris.

"Hmm, I don't know. Both are good fun, I guess. Perhaps the zoo on a sunny day and the art gallery if it's raining? Why? What about you?"

"Oh, we both like them both. How about we pick you up at nine on Saturday, and if it's raining, we'll go to the Beecher Gallery, and if it's sunny, we'll go to the zoo."

Tenealle's heart started beating double time. Wow! A date! Well, sort of a date. "Okay, sure. I'd like that."

"And no extra cousins. Just you and us," added Faris.

"Deal!" Tenealle laughed.

* * * *

The sun was shining brightly, and the forecast was for fine and warm, so Tenealle was dressed for the zoo with her sun hat in her purse, a light sweater knotted around her hips, and comfortable walking shoes on her feet when the doorbell rang.

And there stood Faris, his blond hair and blue eyes accentuated by the deep blue T-shirt he was wearing over his jeans. "Evan is driving, so he sent me to collect you. Are you ready?"

"Sure," she said, grabbing her purse, checking she had her keys, and slamming her door shut. She ran down the steps to the parking lot.

Evan had his car—or maybe it was his and Faris's car—standing at the curb right out front. Faris opened the door and encouraged her to sit on the bench seat between then. Then they were off.

It was a perfect day of warm—but not hot—sunshine, blue skies, and lots to see and do. They licked ice cream cones like kids, *oohed* and *aahhed* at the butterfly house, clowned around outside the monkeys' area, and waited a long time to see and take photographs of a pair of platypuses.

"They're amazing. I've never seen anything like them before," said Tenealle.

"I don't think there is anything else like them," laughed Evan.

"*Ornithorhynchus,* one of the five living species of monotremes, the only mammals that lay eggs instead of giving birth to live young," Faris read from the sign outside the enclosure.

"The bill of a duck, the tail of a beaver, and feet like an otter," said Tenealle. "It's really no wonder scientists thought it was a fraud."

"And it's venomous. That spur on its back foot can do real damage, and delivers a nasty poison," added Evan.

"Well, whatever. I think they're awesome," Tenealle said.

"As good as the butterfly house?" Faris asked.

"Hmm. That's hard. They're both equally special, but in different ways." *Like you. I like you both equally. You're quite different from each other, but match each other so well. I like you both. I want to be with you both.*

There was a moment's silence. Then Evan gently tugged Tenealle into his arms and kissed her. It was a soft, tender, exploratory kiss, but one that thrilled her to her toes. Sweet, but sensual. Undemanding, but hinting, suggesting, there could be so much more.

When they broke apart, Evan said, "We both want you, Tenealle. Do you, could you, want us?"

Faris turned her to him, his eyes pleading. "At least give us a try. Don't say no straightaway."

"I've got no intention of saying no. My answer is an unequivocal yes."

"It is? Excellent. Let's grab some takeout and get you home to our house." Faris hesitated a moment, then added, "Today is okay, isn't it? You weren't meaning next time?"

"No, I wasn't meaning next time. Today is fine. We'll see how it works out."

"Cool! Let's go." Evan grabbed her hand, and they headed back down the path to the exit. At the concession stand, they chose some salads, sandwiches, and sodas, then headed back to the car.

Tenealle was fascinated to see where the men lived. Had her relative left her an apartment, there was no way she would have sold it, so she'd assumed they must live in a largish house and likely in a much nicer neighborhood.

In fact, their apartment was scarcely bigger than hers—two bedrooms, one bath, and a great room.

"Why did you choose to stay here instead of fixing up that apartment you sold me?" she asked Evan.

"Likely it sounds silly, but it just seemed so sad and run-down. I like to remember it from when Great-Uncle Arthur was alive and Great-Aunt Enid used to keep the garden looking beautiful. There were flowers everywhere all year round, and even fish in the fountain. It just seemed like way too much work now to make it look nice when we are happy enough living here. I can invest the money for if I ever need it.

"Now, if we were to find a woman who likes being with two men, then things would be different. A bigger house, maybe even a garden, would be ideal."

Tenealle looked at Evan's worried frown. "It's okay. I see what you mean, and that apartment is perfect for me. I can work from the office section and even have a pullout bed in the outer room for when cousins visit, as well as have the second bedroom set up for guests. And the extra bathroom is awesome. Even Tim might not use all my hot water anymore. Life will be so much easier when they descend on me en masse."

"Why don't you just tell them to get lost?" asked Faris.

"They're family. I love them all. Besides, they know they can only stay a couple of nights before I'll kick them out. And who knows, one day I may travel around and stay at all their places too."

"Uh-huh." Faris moved closer to her. "Let's go eat and build up your strength. It's been a busy day."

Once again, they laughed and joked and relaxed together. Truly, Tenealle had never had such a warm friendship, even with her cousins. It seemed as though she'd known these men forever, not less than a week. But then, they'd spent a lot of time together. Tenealle wondered if some married couples spent eight hours awake together in a week, never mind in a single day.

Almost before the last mouthful of soda was swallowed, Tenealle saw the lust surging in both men's eyes. She gulped in a big breath, noticing how her heart was pounding and cream was flooding her panties. And they hadn't even touched her yet. She'd had a single kiss from Evan—even though it was a very sensual kiss—and nothing more, yet her belly was clenching in need, and her whole being was focused on loving and being loved by these two men.

Two men. Who'd have thought demure, hardworking, ordinary Tenealle Jones would be considering a relationship with two seriously good-looking men? Tall, lean, blond, blue-eyed Faris, with his snarky humor, and dark-haired, muscular Evan, whose apartment had brought them together.

This won't last! her good angel warned her.

Who cares? her bad angel replied. *I enjoy being with them. They're genuinely nice people and good fun to be around. I'm sure the sex will be pretty awesome too!*

Tenealle was by no means a virgin, but she hadn't had very many relationships. Somehow, always being surrounded by a plethora of male cousins had scared away any young men just looking for a one-night stand or an easy girl.

Although many of the cousins were second, third, even fourth cousins, or cousins several times removed, Tenealle was not interested in dating any of them. To her they were all just "cousins" and off-limits for anything more than companionship.

Faris pulled Tenealle into his arms, bringing her mind back to the present. "My turn for a kiss, I believe." His lips touched hers gently, softly, and then they whispered across her cheeks, dropping tiny kisses as they moved. Next, her forehead received his attentions, with more tiny kisses, before his lips moved down to her earlobe. He sucked the lobe into his mouth for a moment, then ran his tongue along the rim of her ear.

A delicious shudder rippled through Tenealle, cranking up the sexual tension. Damn. Once again he'd hardly touched her, but every nerve ending was on fire, and her cunt was throbbing with the need to be filled. *God. All I want is a hot, hard cock pounding into me. Or maybe two cocks. Oh yeah!*

Maybe she had only known them for a week by the calendar, but it seemed to her she knew them through and through. They'd talked for hours on all sorts of subjects. They'd laughed and played and been serious too. So now she was very ready for the next step. Some red-hot sex. God, was she ever ready. Her pussy was dripping cream. Her belly was clenching with need. She was one giant nerve ending throbbing with the desire to be made love to. And she instinctively knew she'd be made love to, not just fucked.

Tenealle wasn't prepared to guess whether or not this relationship would last, but she was certain their time together would be both passionate and fulfilling.

In a single movement, both men pressed into her, Evan's cock against her ass, his muscular body enveloping her from behind, and Faris from the front, his lean length rubbing against her hips, her breasts, and everything in between.

Then she was swept off her feet and carried into the bedroom. She had barely a moment to get an impression of deep blue walls when four hands began to efficiently remove her clothing. She reached out to try to pull Evan's T-shirt over his head, but she was lifted onto the bed, and a deep blue blanket was dropped onto the floor. Then again she was sandwiched between the men, and four hands and two mouths were all over her, licking and sucking, tickling and teasing.

Tenealle pulled her scattered wits together and managed to grab Faris's shirt and tug it upward. He laughed and obligingly ducked his head so she could remove it.

Yum! He had just a slight covering of fair hair across his ripped chest, and she smoothed her hands across the wall of muscle, marveling at how hard his abs were, yet how soft and baby-fine his hair there was.

Naughtily, she tweaked one nipple, and was about to play with the other one, when her own shirt was pulled off and other hands deftly removed her bra. Faris grunted and sucked one of her nipples into his mouth, pressing it up to the roof of his mouth and sending shards of sensation directly from her breast to her cunt.

While Faris moved from one breast to the other and Tenealle ran her fingers through his chest hair, a second pair of hands removed her jeans and panties and nudged her legs wide apart.

Faris shifted his body so he was beside her rather than on top of her, and Evan lay between her legs, his mouth at her pussy, licking the line of her slit. Evan licked all around her clit, but never touched it. He nibbled on her labia, then sucked them into his mouth. He pressed his tongue inside her cunt, imitating what his—or possibly Faris's—cock would be doing later. Then he stroked along the walls of her channel, arousing her to an even higher level of need.

Faris was still concentrating on her breasts. He cupped them in his hands, licked their undersides, sucked the tender skin between them, and teased and tormented her nipples.

Tenealle's heart was pounding, and need was rising to unbearable levels inside her. She writhed under their attentions, and her fingers tightened in Faris's hair, pressing his head to her breasts. "Oh please, I need to come," she begged.

"No, I don't think so," said Evan, lifting his face from her pussy, the gleam of her juices glowing around his mouth.

"What the hell—" began Tenealle.

"Every time we hold you back, make you wait, you will start again, more aroused than before, and rise even higher. The longer you wait for your orgasm, the better it will be when you eventually come," added Faris.

"But I want…I need…"

"Trust us," said Evan, sliding all the way down her body to her toes. Tenderly, he blew warm air on each one, then licked lines around her heels, under her arches, circling her ankles. And every time he blew on the damp places, it sent shivers of delight through her body.

Faris was still absorbed in teasing her breasts. He licked circles around her nipples. Then, like Evan, he blew on the wet skin, sending more shivers through her body. He tongue-painted wet patterns between and around her breasts, lines, curves, and spirals, and everything he did aroused her more.

Tenealle dug her fingers into his hair, stroking his ears with her thumbs, as tension and need kept rising and rising inside her until she thought she might explode.

Evan kneeled between her legs, and finally—finally!—his cock slid into her hungry, aching cunt. At once Tenealle felt so full, so stretched, so complete. But not satisfied. She wanted more. She wanted him pounding inside her, bringing them both to completion.

But what about Faris?

As if he was connected to her thoughts, Faris slid his leg over her waist and kneeled over her in front of Evan. Faris held her breasts together and slid his huge, hot, hard cock into the valley he'd created.

His strokes kept pace with Evan's, and Tenealle was overwhelmed with the sensations of two cocks making love to her at once, two men holding her, loving her.

She wrapped her legs around Evan's hips, matching his thrusts, and her hands rested on Faris's hips, holding him tightly as his cock pushed up between her breasts. She stretched her neck forward and flicked her tongue over the head of his cock as it completed its forward stroke, then maintained the rhythm, her hips moving with Evan, her upper body keeping time with Faris.

But it was far too good, far too intense, far too beautiful an experience for her mind to grasp right now. All she could do was feel, enjoy, and accept the tension rising, rising, rising inside her.

The men increased their pace, and Tenealle's heart pounded with the urgent need to come. She leaned forward to lick Faris's cock, but the men's thrusts were coming so fast now, she barely got a taste of him each time.

And then she was there. The orgasm burst out of her with a blaze of feeling, her cunt pulsing in release, her ankles locking hard around Evan's waist, her toes curling back toward her soles, her fingers digging into Faris's shoulders of their own volition.

She felt an extra burst of heat in her pussy and knew Evan had come, his thrusts growing ragged for a few strokes as his hot cum filled the condom.

Faris held her breasts firmly, pinching her nipples, and more waves of orgasm flashed through Tenealle. She opened her mouth just as his seed burst out in long, white, ropey streams from between her breasts. She caught some of it on her tongue, enjoying his tart, spicy flavor.

The two men withdrew from her, then rolled onto their sides, sandwiching her tightly between them, their arms wrapped around each other, holding her firmly pressed against them both.

"Rest now. Then we'll do it again," said Evan.

"Again, huh? Well, this time, can I be on top?" she asked.

"On top? How do you plan to do that?" asked Faris.

"Hmm. Well you could lie side by side on your backs, and I could sit across your legs and play with your cocks," she suggested.

"Play how?" asked Evan.

"Oh, I'm sure I'll think of something." She grinned naughtily, her head buried against Evan's chest so they couldn't see her face. She inhaled deeply, loving his spicy, slightly sweaty scent.

"Well I think we'd all better have a shower first. Some of us are slightly sticky," said Faris, slapping Evan's arm and half pulling Tenealle upright.

The shower was not big, but all three of them did fit under the water together. The men kept Tenealle in the middle of them, and while one was shampooing her hair, the other was rubbing shower gel over her back, her arms, and her legs.

Tenealle tried to reciprocate, but no sooner did she get her hands on one man, than she was rotated and found herself facing the other.

After a lot of splashing, and some pushing and shoving, mostly by Tenealle, they were all soaped, rinsed, and wrapped in large, soft, fluffy towels in a deep blue shade Tenealle liked.

She couldn't help but notice both men's cocks were ready for action again. Evan's penis was wider and a slightly darker color than Faris's—like his body, his cock was long. But Tenealle had no complaints about Evan's equipment. He'd filled and stretched her pussy in the most delicious way and given her an excellent orgasm.

"Now lie on your backs and let me play," she ordered them.

"What do you plan to play?"asked Faris curiously.

"I'll think of something," she replied, moving over to a large chest of drawers. The first drawer held socks and briefs, which she ignored. But the second had neckties and other male accessories she rather thought could be fun.

Tenealle grabbed a handful of neckties and gently bound their hands together, then tied the two men together by using a few neckties to loop their manacled hands together.

Then she settled herself over their four legs and draped a couple of neckties over their bodies, swirling the fabric across their abs, around their belly buttons, and over their thighs. Both cocks lengthened and darkened with need, and already a bead of cum had formed in the eye of Faris's cock.

"I must be doing something right," she murmured.

"Ah, honey, you're killing us here," said Evan.

Faris nodded and wiggled his hips.

Tenealle rubbed her wet pussy up and down their thighs, then rotated herself to sit across their bellies so they couldn't see what she was doing.

She tormented them, gently stroking their thighs and groins, even occasionally touching their balls or shafts very lightly, but never giving satisfaction.

By now both men were frantically thrusting their hips up at her, desperate for fulfillment. Tenealle decided she had teased them enough. Besides, she was longing for a taste of them both.

She gripped a cock firmly in each hand, sliding her fist up from root to tip, reveling in the sensations of strong muscles inside soft skin. Again and again she stroked them, adding an occasional twist to her grip, before leaning forward to suck first Evan, then Faris, deep into her mouth.

Next, she played with their balls, rolling them inside their sacs while licking across the cock heads. Finally, she settled down to seriously suck them, a hand on each shaft, holding it firmly and stroking it while she sucked first one, then the other, rubbing along the thick, ropey vein, running her tongue under the sensitive ridge of the caps, and scraping her teeth gently over the two cock heads.

Tenealle was enjoying herself very much, concentrating on pleasing her men, loving the urgent upthrusts of their hips, when four hands grabbed her and flipped her over. A condom appeared from nowhere, and Faris was pushing deep into her cunt.

"What the hell?" Her brain was reeling with the sudden change of game plan.

"We untied each other. It's time for us to take charge," said Evan, kneeling beside her head and offering his red and needy cock to her lips.

Faris held her hips still while she opened wide to accept as much of Evan into her mouth as she could take. Tenealle tipped her head right back, opening the back of her throat, and swallowed his cock head.

God, he felt good, and so did Faris in her pussy. When Faris pushed right in, he almost touched the mouth of her womb, he was so long.

The two men controlled their strokes, pushing in and pulling out simultaneously, quickly driving Tenealle to a place where she lost all power to think and could barely remember to vary her sucking to give Evan pleasure. Faster and faster the men thrust, pushing into her hard and deep. Tenealle clenched her pussy muscles and sucked hard, running her tongue under the ridge of Evan's cock.

Fingers pinched her nipples. A fingernail scraped across her clit, and an orgasm exploded from her pussy, her clit, her breasts. The power of her climax made Tenealle shake all over. Desperately she sucked on Evan, wanting him to come too. Again she ran her tongue under the sensitive cap of his penis, then pressed her tongue along the vein of his shaft, rubbing up and down, before sucking him as deep as she could once again.

Suddenly, both men were there, Faris exploding in her hot pussy, and Evan in her mouth. Quickly she swallowed, enjoying his salty taste, and unbelievably, as she did, ripples spread from her pussy throughout her body.

She licked Evan clean, then relaxed back into the bed, feeling completed, fulfilled, satisfied.

"Damn, you two are good," she whispered after Evan pulled out of her mouth.

"You're pretty good yourself, honey," said Faris, rolling her onto her side so both men could snuggle into her.

Tenealle was about to reply, but before her mouth could form the words, she was instantly, deeply asleep.

Chapter Three

Evan and Faris had made it very plain they wanted to spend a lot more time with Tenealle, and she wanted that too, but she needed to concentrate on her job. One of the downsides of working from home as a subcontractor was that, because she was at home during the day, people thought she was free to do things, but that simply meant she had to make up those work hours in the evenings. If she didn't work, she didn't earn any money—quite apart from pissing off her boss and colleagues who had to pick up the slack—and besides, right now she needed every dollar she could earn to pay off her new apartment.

Tenealle spent three full days working like a fiend, completing half-done projects, sending out paperwork and guidelines for potential new carers, and catching up on tasks. Then, when Faris rang for the third time in three days—not counting the four calls from Evan she'd also received—she agreed to go out to dinner with them.

"Where would you like to go? What type of food do you prefer?" asked Faris.

"Something simple. I don't want to have to spend an hour getting dressed," she replied, then wondered if that made her sound like a cheap, lazy tart. But it was the truth. She was just as happy wearing jeans and eating fries as she was at a formal dinner, dressed up in her best clothes and likely eating pommes frites.

"Oh, good. Neither of us is eager to wear a necktie around you, after your devilish use of them. Shall we pick you up at seven then?"

"That'll be great. See you both then."

Tenealle was dressed in black jeans and a figure-hugging black T-shirt when the men arrived. She liked wearing jeans, as it meant she had enough pockets to carry everything she'd need for the evening, so she wouldn't have to worry about bringing a purse. *Although a spare pair of panties might be useful.*

Faris rang her doorbell at exactly 7:00 p.m., and she assumed Evan would be waiting in their—his?—car out front. But it wasn't a car. It was a horse and carriage.

"Up you get," said Faris, giving her a boost onto the high seat where Evan was waiting, holding the horse's reins lightly in his hands.

Tenealle scrambled up onto the seat, then slid over to make room for Faris. "Wow! This is awesome," she gasped as Evan flicked the reins and the horse ambled off.

Tenealle was entranced. The city looked totally different from a horse and carriage. They moved at walking pace, so she had plenty of time to see everything as they passed by. Although there was a hood sort of thing over them, not being inside a vehicle gave her a feeling of being at one with the streetscape and everything they saw. Aromas were stronger, more immediate, the smells of people's suppers cooking wafting from their apartments, the sap from the trees and the scents of the flowers. Colors seemed brighter, more vivid. It was like seeing the streets for the very first time all over again.

When they arrived at the restaurant, Tenealle asked, "How do you park this thing? What happens to the horse while we're inside?"

Evan waved at an elderly man standing on the sidewalk. "He drives the horse and carriage back to their stable. We'll go home by more conventional means."

"Makes sense." Tenealle nodded, trying to scramble down with some semblance of grace and, in particular, not fall flat on her ass. "I really enjoyed the ride. We seemed so much more part of the neighborhood moving at a slow pace like that. It's a totally different experience from walking around or traveling by car."

The men grinned at each other, then guided her inside.

"So let's eat," said Faris prosaically.

They ordered a range of dishes to share, then while they were waiting for their salads, Tenealle asked, "However did you think of something so different as the horse and carriage?"

"We wanted the evening to be special for you—" began Faris.

"And you liked the zoo, so we assumed a horse wouldn't frighten you," added Evan.

"I like animals. I've never had a pet of my own, but once I move into my new apartment, I'll be able to have a small dog because it can play in the courtyard. Or maybe a cat, although I guess it may climb over the wall and get lost."

"A dog would be safer," agreed Faris.

"What breed are you thinking of?" asked Evan.

"Oh, I'll adopt one from the animal shelter. They'll be able to tell me which ones are temperamentally suited to apartment living and not having other dogs to play with. I also want one that won't grow too big, and even with mixed parentage dogs, they'll be able to tell me that, too."

The conversation roamed through the attitudes and abilities of various types of dogs, the relative advantages of dogs over cats, then to various other animals while they ate their salads and drank a glass each of a full-bodied Italian red wine. Then they shared out their choices of dishes and continued eating.

Faris had them both laughing with his story of a childhood adventure riding an elephant, which had made a habit of picking the pockets of those waiting in line. Then the conversation turned to interior decorating.

"So what do you plan to do first with your new home?" asked Evan curiously.

"Well, I hope you won't be upset, Evan. I really want to get the garden cleaned up and the fountain working properly again. My cousin, Jodie, Mark's sister, studied horticulture, and she's willing to advise me and help me. And I have plenty of able-bodied male cousins to provide the unskilled labor. I'll wash down all the walls myself, then get some cousins around to help me paint. After the painting I'll organize floor coverings. But I need to fix the garden first so they don't track dirt all over my new rugs."

"That sounds logical. And don't worry about hurting my feelings. I'll be very happy to see it all restored and looking good again. I just didn't have the heart to do it myself. Or the cousins to provide the physical labor," he added, grinning.

The conversation wandered through the comparative merits of tiles, polished wood, rugs, and carpets as floor coverings. The men even discussed color schemes, which surprised Tenealle, as she couldn't think of any male cousins who'd tolerate such a topic at the dinner table.

They'd drunk their coffee and it was time to go before Tenealle looked at her watch and was astounded to see it was nearly midnight. "Good heavens! How did it get so late? I'll never get up in time for my seven o'clock online meeting tomorrow morning."

"Seven o'clock?" queried Evan.

"Yes, we have a regular 'staff meeting' in a chat room. I need to keep the work rolling in to pay for this new apartment, you know."

"We can't keep calling it 'the new apartment.' You really should invent some sort of a name for it," said Evan as they walked into the parking lot.

"Like what?"

"Tenealle's Courtyard?"

"The Garden Abode" was Faris's suggestion.

"Tenealle's Domain?"

"Hmm. That's not bad, Evan. But how about just The Domain? I like that."

"The Domain it is."

As they climbed into Evan's car, Tenealle asked, "How did your car get here?"

"We had the man from the horse-and-carriage place drive it here. He had to meet us here, and we had to get home, so it seemed to be the easiest solution, really," said Faris.

There was a moment's silence, and then Evan asked, "Will you come home with us tonight? I know it's late and you said you have to work tomorrow, but we really want to make love to you again."

Tenealle's breath hitched at the emotion in his voice. *Damn, but I want that, too. They love me so thoroughly, arouse me so instantly, I can't see them without wanting more. And I really do want more.*

"Yes, I'd like that. I want both of you inside me together," she said, blushing furiously.

"Oh, honey, we want that, too. But we didn't want to rush you. Are you sure you're ready for that?" asked Evan.

"It's the most intense experience. For you and for us," added Faris.

"Yes. It's what I want."

The sexual tension in the car was as thick as fog. Hoarsely, Faris said, "Thank you, honey. You will enjoy it beyond anything, we promise you."

Oh yeah, she knew she would. They were both very considerate lovers, always giving far more than they took, always seeking to ensure her pleasure.

Despite only having had a few relationships, Tenealle had experienced and enjoyed anal sex. It was quite different from vaginal sex, yet just as pleasurable. There were so many nerve endings around the anus, arousal was pretty much guaranteed.

Both men slung their arms across her shoulders, wrapping her between them as they walked into their apartment. Then Evan picked her up. "Evan carry woman to cave."

Tenealle laughed. Faris pushed past them, saying, "Faris prepare cave for woman."

Evan spun around and around, until Tenealle was almost dizzy, before dropping her onto the bed. Faris had indeed prepared the "cave" with soft orchestral music coming from the sound system, one lamp lit in the corner of the room, providing a dim, romantic atmosphere, and several tea lights glowing on the windowsill, giving off a gentle cinnamon fragrance.

"Nice cave," murmured Tenealle.

"Woman not naked yet," replied Evan.

"Men not naked yet, either." She half sat up on the bed to reach for Evan's shirt. He lightly smacked her hands away so he could unfasten her jeans. Faris was at the other end of the bed, pulling her shoes and socks off.

In moments she was naked, lying on her front, and four hands were teasing her ass, stroking and patting her spine and her butt, before a slippery finger slid into her hole, smoothing cool gel all around inside.

Tenealle sighed with delight at the feelings the men were invoking. Already the sexual tension was rising again after their lighthearted play, and the hands on her skin were incredibly arousing. A second finger slid into her ass, and the two fingers began stretching as well as stroking the tissues, widening her, loosening the muscles, making her ready for a cock.

Her pussy was weeping with need. She was ready, so very ready, for them both. "I need you both now," she said, pushing up into their hands.

One pair of hands continued to pat and stroke her, while the other body, Faris, jumped off the bed and his clothes flew across the room.

Then he was rolling a condom onto his penis, lying on his back, and pulling Tenealle over to himself. "Climb aboard, honey." He ground his cock against her pussy.

By the time Faris was fully seated inside her, Evan had returned to the bed with his hands resting on her spine, pushing her body down flat on Faris to raise her ass toward himself.

Evan pressed his cock into her dark channel. The head nudged her opening, pushed against the ring, then popped through the relaxed muscles. He moved slowly, gradually, inching in, and Tenealle felt her tissues spread to accept him. She had felt completely filled with only Faris inside her, but as Evan joined him, her channels widened to accept them both, and soon both men were incredibly deep inside her, filling her to the brim. For a few moments the three held quite still, all of them adjusting to the erotic sensations. Then both men pulled out together, almost all the way, leaving just the heads of their cocks inside her, before pressing in again. Then out, and in, increasing the pace and force.

They held Tenealle tightly between them, scarcely allowing her to move. Her body was on sensory overload, and she wouldn't have known what to do anyway. The friction was delicious, the feeling of fullness exquisite. Being surrounded, enveloped, possessed by two men at once was indescribably good.

Tenealle managed to squeeze her internal muscles and was rewarded with two harsh groans from her men.

Faris nudged her chin up a little higher and took her mouth in a deep, possessive kiss. His tongue thrust in and out, matching the movements of the two cocks lower down. Then Evan's mouth was on her neck and shoulders, licking and sucking there.

Tenealle broke off the kiss to gasp for breath, and continued gasping as the men's powerful strokes had her cresting fast into an orgasm. Then her body exploded. The climax roared through her, making her ass clench on Evan while her cunt was rippling and milking Faris. Her arms and legs stiffened and jerked as wave after wave of release rolled through her body, only gradually decreasing in power.

"Damn, you're both good. I've never come so hard in my life before," she whispered hoarsely.

"But you will again," promised Evan.

"Hell yeah," agreed Faris.

* * * *

The men insisted on feeding her breakfast before they took her home, and they all got sidetracked for a little while in the shower, so it was actually five minutes after seven before Tenealle slid into her office chair and logged into the chat room.

At ten she logged out and checked her e-mail. The first one she opened was from Cousin Herb, reminding her about the party for Emma on Saturday. He also hinted that he expected her to bring two guests.

The men had been present when Herb had talked about Emma's party, but she had no idea if they'd been aware of what the conversation was about, so she jotted down a note to invite them, and a second note to herself to check if she was supposed to bring some food or drinks for the cookout.

Then she dived into dealing with her work e-mails. She loved her job, loved the actual work, the feeling of matching pieces of a puzzle together, loved the freedom it gave her, but she really needed to concentrate on making some money.

She'd also been e-mailing backward and forward with Jodie about the garden. Jodie had some detailed plans that looked really good. Tenealle was excited by the idea that the garden would look truly beautiful again, and Jodie didn't think achieving this would be expensive.

Then there were her plans to renovate the Domain. Nothing structural needed fixing, just paint for the walls, new drapes for the windows, minor carpentry, and basic upkeep, then finally new floor coverings, possibly mostly tiles and rugs. *This could be the one time that having a bazillion cousins is actually helpful,* she thought before deliberately putting the Domain aside to concentrate on the work that would pay the bills for it.

* * * *

"How do you feel about attending this party for Tenealle's cousin Emma?" Faris asked Evan as they were getting ready to pick Tenealle up.

"I think it'll be good to meet some of these bazillion cousins. Herbert seems an all right kind of guy. Besides, it's pretty obvious she loves them all, even if she does whine up a storm about them at times."

"I guess it cramps her style to trip over family on every street corner. But they've already done us a good turn. If there wasn't so many of them, she'd never have wanted a bigger apartment," said Faris thoughtfully.

"Yeah. Definitely a win for us there."

"What if we're all still together after she's fixed up the apartment? How will you feel about that?"

"You know, I don't think that will matter at all. It's more I couldn't bear it so run-down and sad-looking. Her living in it and making it nice again won't worry me. I really think the three of us will be together for a while yet, and she definitely needs a bigger place. Do you think she'd mind if we bought her a big new bed to christen the place with?" asked Evan.

"I dunno. Females can be weird about that sort of stuff. Better to wait and see."

Although they'd been told no gifts were necessary, as it wasn't that kind of party, since the party was specifically for Emma, they'd decided that bringing flowers was a safe bet. Then they'd wondered if that would hurt Tenealle's feelings, so they'd bought a bunch for her as well.

Promptly at noon they presented themselves and flower bunch number one at Tenealle's home.

"Oh, they're lovely, thank you. And don't you both look good enough to eat as well," she said, her dark chocolate eyes glowing with lust as her gaze took in their neatly pressed jeans and chest-hugging

T-shirts, Faris's blue like his eyes and Evan's a deep green that complemented his dark hair.

"You look pretty damn delicious yourself," Faris responded, his gaze absorbing her long legs under the short denim skirt, and the effect of her reddish-brown hair falling loosely onto the shoulders of her pale blue collared top.

"Hell yeah. I don't suppose we have time for a quickie before we leave?" Evan asked hopefully, licking his lips as his eyes ate her up.

Tenealle laughed and shook her head. "Absolutely not. But you are a very tempting pair."

Not half as tempting as you, thought Faris, his cock achingly hard and throbbing against his zipper.

A quick glance showed him Evan was just as aroused. "Damn. We'll be walking like penguins all afternoon, you look so hot." Faris took her hand to led her out to the car.

* * * *

Herbert's house was on a large block of land with extensive gardens, a big swimming pool, and hot tub off the back deck.

A barbecue pit was smoking out back, with long tables nearby, laden with salads, plates, and cold drinks. Herbert's wife, Delores, had encouraged everyone to leave their shoes on the back deck, as she didn't want to damage the new tiles around the pool. It all sounded totally weird to Faris, but several people were commenting how it reminded them of Europe, and not being allowed to wear shoes on the marble floors of buildings there, so he just shrugged and carried his, Evan's, and Tenealle's shoes over to the collection on the deck.

"I hope we can find our own shoes to wear when it's time to leave."

"Mine aren't anything special. I might end up with a much nicer pair," Tenealle joked.

The food was yummy, the company pleasant, the sun shone brightly, and Faris found himself enjoying the party and Tenealle's myriad cousins. They seemed a pretty normal bunch, and entertaining to talk to, although he had to acknowledge it was unusual to go to a party where almost everyone seemed to be related to everyone else. He was also totally confused about the reason for the party. He'd assumed it was for her graduation—hadn't Herbert said something about her being almost graduated?—but she had not quite finished her studies, and it wasn't her birthday, and she didn't seem to be engaged to the young man with her whose name he couldn't remember. But he guessed it wouldn't be smart to ask Tenealle any leading questions until they got home.

Around 6:00 p.m., people started to leave, so they said their goodbyes and collected their shoes. Tenealle slipped hers on, then stood talking to Herb, Delores, and Emma for a brief moment.

Tenealle slid her feet out of her shoes again.

"What's wrong?" asked Faris.

"I don't know. My feet are burning. They feel really strange."

Mark, the huge cousin, grabbed Tenealle, threw her over his shoulder, then tossed her into the swimming pool, yelling, "That'll cool you down. I've been wanting to throw someone in all day."

Faris raced over to the pool, but Tenealle was just standing there, shaking water out of her hair and laughing. "Damn you, Mark. I'll get you for that one day!"

Evan looked like he wanted to punch Mark, and Faris felt much the same, but since Tenealle was holding her sides and laughing, he figured starting a fight wasn't the right way to respond.

Evan must have disagreed with Faris's logic. He hip-and-shouldered Mark, who was still standing on the edge of the pool, and the big man fell in with a mountainous splash.

Some of the younger cousins started screaming as the water drenched them, and within moments, bodies were flying through the air, and the pool was filling up with fully clad people, most of them laughing uproariously.

Tenealle climbed out of the pool. "Unless you two fancy a swim, I think now would be a good time to leave."

Faris grabbed Tenealle, Evan picked up her shoes, Herb handed her a pool towel to wrap around herself, and they walked back down the long driveway to the street, where they'd parked the car.

"Come on, honey. Let's get you out of those wet things," said Faris.

"Oh yeah. Sounds like a very good plan," added Evan.

"Men. One-track minds." Tenealle was still laughing.

"My hand is hurting," said Evan, stopping in the middle of the path.

"What?"

"My hand," Evan repeated, swapping Tenealle's shoes into his other hand to look at his sore hand carefully. "My fingers are burning."

"Damn. Has one of my idiot cousins put itching powder in everyone's shoes or something?"

"Not itching. Burning," said Evan, dropping her shoes and running back up the driveway toward the house.

Tenealle bent down to pick up her shoes, but Faris stopped her. "Don't touch them." He squatted down and looked carefully inside her shoes. He could see a very faint trace of powder or something on the insides. He pulled off his T-shirt, wrapped her shoes in it, then settled her in the car wrapped in her towel and put the shoes in the trunk.

"Are your feet hot?" she asked.

"Nope." He kicked off a shoe and looked inside it. "Looks and feels perfectly normal to me."

"Just one of the younger cousins being silly then."

"Well I don't know. Evan didn't hold your shoes for very long before he felt his fingers burning."

"I hope he's okay. Should we go back and check on him?"

"He's coming now," said Faris, watching in the rearview mirror.

"Are you okay?" they chorused as Evan got in the car.

"Yeah, I just washed my hands thoroughly. We need to check what's in her shoes, though. If it was meant as a joke, it's not very funny."

There was a few moments' silence as Faris turned the car around and they headed for his and Evan's apartment.

"I didn't want to seem like a moron there, but what exactly were we celebrating?"

"It was a party for Emma. I thought I explained that. And you bought her flowers," Tenealle replied, confused.

"Yeah, we got that. But why? Why was Emma having a party?" asked Evan.

"Oh. Because she's pretty much finished college. She just has a couple of classes to finalize. Then she'll graduate."

"So won't there be a party when she graduates?" Faris was even more puzzled now.

"Of course she'll have a graduation party."

"So why the party today? I don't get it."

"Herb and Delores love throwing parties. Emma is excited by almost being finished school. It seemed a good enough reason."

Faris and Evan looked at each other, eyebrows raised. Finally Evan said, "Your family is weird."

"Absolutely! I thought you already knew that."

They all laughed. And Faris realized they did that a lot. With Tenealle around, happiness was guaranteed, and lots of laughter was part of the package.

But he would definitely get the powder in her shoes analyzed. One of her cousins needed a slap upside the head, and he was just the man to deliver it.

Chapter Four

The final paperwork was signed, and the Domain was officially Tenealle's. She summoned a horde of cousins, who helped her move into her new home, *oohed* and *aahed* over it, told her how to fix it, ate a ton of pizzas, then left.

By the end of the day, the pizza delivery boy was Tenealle's newest best friend, her possessions were all where she wanted them, her bedroom walls had been washed, sanded, filled, and painted with two coats of sea green paint. Matching sea green drapes hung at the sparkling clean windows, overlooking a courtyard garden that had been pruned, weeded, swept, and the fountain had been scrubbed clean and refilled.

"Did your aunt have any trouble with cats getting the fish in her fountain?" Tenealle asked Evan.

"No. As far as I know, the fish only ever died of natural causes. I know you said you thought a cat might get out and get lost, but that wall is very high and sheer, with no way to climb it, so I don't think it's very likely. But then, if you have a cat of your own, you'd need to cover the fountain to protect your fish. If you decide to have fish," was Evan's rather rambling reply.

"I'd rather have a little dog than a cat, but I will have fish in the fountain. It's kind of crazy, but it's my kind of crazy. I like the idea," she replied.

Faris had been waiting until they were alone, not just to test-drive the new king-size bed the three of them had purchased together a week ago, but also to tell her the results of the analysis on her shoes. She'd never mentioned her shoes, although she had to realize he'd never given them back to her. Plus, he and Evan had kept a close watch on all the cousins today. The last thing they wanted was any more strange powders in her bedding, clothes, or food. Fortunately the cousins had worked in teams, with no one alone for more than a few seconds, as groups of them had banded together to fetch, carry, clean, paint, and garden.

But now, he didn't quite know how to broach the subject. "Um, honey, about your shoes…"

"Ah, I wondered when you'd get around to talking about that. It was just my imagination, wasn't it?"

"No, not quite."

"Well, what then?"

"Drain cleaner," Faris and Evan said together.

"Drain cleaner?" she echoed.

"Yep. Very caustic. Will burn your skin quite nastily. But not poisonous unless swallowed."

"Well I was hardly likely to lick the inside my shoes, was I?"

"Oooh, kinky! Seriously, one of your cousins needs a reality check. It was a pretty stupid thing to do."

"I wonder if it was even meant for me. Maybe they mistook my shoes for someone else's. After all, there were a lot of shoes in that pile," she said thoughtfully.

"I guess that's possible. But I agree with Faris. It was a stupid thing to do, and the culprit needs to be caught and slapped some."

"But how could we find out? Everyone left their shoes in the pile, then picked them up. It could be anyone."

"Not quite. It had to be someone who knew which shoes were yours. Who was standing around watching when we arrived?" asked Evan.

"It's weeks ago. How would I know now? And they may have mistaken my shoes for someone else's anyway."

"Let's assume for the moment that they deliberately targeted you. Come on, try to remember. Herbert and Delores were greeting the guests. Emma was out by the barbecue pit."

Tenealle frowned for a moment, obviously thinking. "There was a group of younger guys over on one side. Herb didn't bother to introduce you to them. One was Emma's boyfriend, Steve, and there was Jodie's boyfriend, Clint, and a couple of others. Younger cousins. Let me think. Oh, of course, it was Nate and Nick, the Terrible Twosome. Yeah, well, they're ripe for mischief for sure."

"See how easy that was? Now, I think it's time to christen your new bedroom. You aren't too tired, are you?" Faris was suddenly aware that it had been a long day, and maybe he was pushing her.

"I'm never too tired for you two. But I think we need a good shower first."

"Not a problem. A horde of girl cousins had your bathroom shiny clean hours ago. Let's go then," said Evan.

The bathroom was indeed clean, but sadly in need of retiling. "You know, I think I'll pull out the fixtures and put a Jacuzzi in here. The room is plenty big enough for that, as well as a sink and toilet, and there's a shower in the small bathroom off the office."

"Oh yeah, a Jacuzzi. That does sound good. But meanwhile, this shower will work just fine to get the sweat off us," said Faris.

"Uh-huh. Then you'll make me sweaty all over again," she laughed.

"That's the plan." Faris's cock was harder than the tiles on the floor. His pants suddenly felt way too tight, and he had to unzip them slowly for fear he'd do himself an injury. Finally his cock sprang free of the confining jeans, but that was no relief. She'd peeled her shirt off, and one glance at those luscious breasts of hers had his damn dick throbbing even harder.

Faris looked at Evan. Evan had one leg out of his jeans, and his tongue was about hanging out as he looked at Faris's cock. Evan's cock was huge, too, and ready for action.

Faris looked at Evan again and raised an eyebrow, hoping his partner understood he wanted to be the middle of the ménage this time. Evan's slight nod seemed to imply he had.

Faris hurried to rip the rest of his clothes off and get his hands on delicious Tenealle. *God, that woman is hot. And always so ready and willing for us no matter what games we want to play. I think I love—no. No way. I'm not going there! It's way too soon for that.*

Evan had set the water running and grabbed condoms for them both. Faris rifled through the sink drawer for the lube and briefly wondered what the girl cousins had thought about that.

Then all three of them were in the shower, under the water, and sharing in a group hug. The three-way kiss was sloppy and made even sloppier by the warm water spraying down over them all. Their mouths and noses meshed together, tongues flicking in and out of each others' mouths, arms and hands gripping and patting whoever they could reach.

But Faris was way too desperate to fuck and be fucked to spend very long playing. He turned Tenealle to the wall, and she instantly braced herself on her forearms, pushing her ass out toward him and watching the two men over her shoulder.

Faris hastily took a condom from Evan and rolled it down his cock, wishing he'd had the forethought to do it before he got under the water, as he noticed Evan had done. Ah well, too bad. He certainly wasn't going to take the time to dry his penis now, and it rolled on okay anyway.

Damn, Tenealle looked hot leaning against the tile wall and watching over her shoulder, her beautiful red-brown hair turning a darker shade as it became wet. He could see one lovely, plump breast, but it was her ass that drew his gaze. It was round and pert, and totally delicious. Gently, he smoothed a hand across her ass cheek, enjoying the silky feeling of her soft skin kissed by water droplets. He let his hand explore across her hip, then around her groin, and at last his fingers sank into her pussy.

Hot, so hot. And tight. So very tight. He couldn't wait a moment longer. He rested his hand across her mons, the fingers along her slit, and used his other hand to guide his aching, throbbing cock deep inside her welcoming pussy. Oh yes. That felt so very, very good.

Faris pushed deep inside Tenealle, until his balls were hard against her upper thighs and his belly rested against her luscious ass. He nuzzled her neck and kissed her jawline, then pressed his finger on her clit as he spread his legs and braced himself to accept Evan.

He knew Evan was as needy and anxious as he was, so guessed there wouldn't be much preparation of his ass. But it didn't worry him. He didn't mind the bite of pain with his pleasure from time to time, and his cock was aching, burning to get moving.

Tenealle was waggling her hips and pressing back into him, so he was pleased to feel a slippery finger invade his ass. Holding Tenealle hard against him with a hand on her hip, he pressed them both back into Evan's finger.

He smelled a girly, flowery scent and realized that the lube may have been provided by the female cousins, but couldn't care. At least it covered up the pervading aroma of cleaning products and bleach. Then Evan was teasing and tormenting his ass, pressing the gel into the walls of his rectum and widening his channel.

Faris kept Tenealle pressed to him, but she was wiggling and driving him mad with the urge to pump into her. The double torment of being inside her and having Evan's fingers inside himself was destroying the last vestiges of his control.

"Enough! Just do it," he groaned.

"About time," said Tenealle, trying to escape his hold.

Finally Evan pressed inside him, and he had to count backward by threes from fifty to stop himself coming on the spot. Evan's hands rested on his hips, and together he and Evan withdrew, then plunged back in, pulled out, and pushed in, getting a synchronized rhythm going.

Evan moved one hand from Faris's hip to Tenealle's waist, while Faris kept his hand on Tenealle's clit and rotated the other back to grab Evan's butt. Tenealle rested her head on the tiles and wrapped both her arms backward as far as she could reach, enclosing the three of them into a unit.

Faris didn't know whether it was water from the shower or sweat, but his body was hot and slick as Evan jackhammered in and out of him and he pistoned into Tenealle in the same time and rhythm, keeping in beat with Evan. They were ramping up the pace, moving faster and faster, thrusting harder and deeper.

Tenealle was panting against the wall, and he slid his fingers along her slit. He could already feel the rippling beginnings of her orgasm grabbing at his cock.

His balls were pulled up hard and tight against his body, and his spine had started to tingle. No amount of control could hold off his orgasm much longer.

Then Evan gave a shout, and Faris felt a flood of heat in his ass as Evan came. He relaxed his control and pinched Tenealle's clit. They both came together, his cock pumping jet after jet of cum into the condom in her, and her cunt rippling and milking him as Evan's cock still spurted into his ass.

The three relaxed against each other for a moment, all panting. Then the men withdrew and got rid of their condoms before pulling Tenealle in for a group hug, sandwiching her in the middle of them this time.

"That was unbelievable. I could feel everything. Every pulse from Evan into Faris was transferred from him to me. It was awesome, just awesome," she said, leaning into their arms. "And the shower water hasn't even run cold yet. Ha! That'll be perfect next time Tim visits."

Tim? Faris didn't have a clue what she was talking about. But who cared? His man and his woman were both in his arms, and life was very, very good.

* * * *

"I think I might call Adam Titus today and talk to him about following through on that drain cleaner thing," Evan said, flicking a look at Faris as he drove them both to work.

"Why talk to him? About what in particular?"

"Well I can't exactly go up to Tenealle's cousins and tell them they need a punch in the face, can I? But I can't let it rest either. What if one of the idiots tries to hurt her again? Even worse, what if they succeed? It'd kill me if she was hurt."

"Yeah," agreed Faris. "It'd kill me, too. But I reckon she's going to get hurt anyway when she understands one of her cousins really did try to harm her. I don't think she believes that at all, as yet."

"You're right. For all her grumbling, she loves the whole goddamn pack of them. Seventy-two cousins. Sheesh!"

"But that's what makes it so weird. Why hurt her? Why her out of the entire crowd? You don't think it's anything to do with us, do you? Some moral campaigner among the cousins?"

"No. Those young guys didn't strike me as moral puritans, judging by the looks they were giving the girls, and their language," replied Evan.

"It probably wouldn't hurt to find out a bit more about the ones she called the Terrible Twosome. Nate and Nick, wasn't it? She seemed to think they were ripe for mischief."

"Yeah. Sounds like a plan. I just hope she doesn't think I'm spying on her, that's all."

* * * *

Tenealle had found the only way to keep her work hours up, and make steady progress on fixing up the Domain, was to be very organized and focused. Since she was a scheduler, that worked best for her. She was at her desk, ready to work, at seven a.m. every day and kept her butt firmly in her chair until ten. Then she spent an hour doing chores and was back at work until one. She took her lunch break and spent an hour either planning her renovations, doing something herself, or pricing and choosing things. Frequently her lunch was eaten at her computer as she Googled furnishings, fabrics, or home project advice sites.

From three until five thirty, she was back at her day job. Then it was time to get ready for whatever Evan and Faris had planned for the evening.

Tenealle giggled to herself. She wondered if they'd realized yet just how often the activities she chose fit into her home improvement plans. Still, every evening ended up most satisfactorily in bed, so they couldn't complain.

It was just after six, and she was showered and ready for the men to pick her up. She'd actually talked them into going to a home show tonight. A group of home improvement stores had hired a convention center and filled it with bathroom designs and furnishings, and Tenealle wanted to look at the various different kinds of hot tubs. She wasn't sure whether Evan and Faris simply hadn't been paying attention when she'd suggested getting tickets for the show, or whether they were thinking of "show" as in "movie," but either way she was looking forward to both the bathrooms on display and the men's expressions when they saw inside the building.

Tenealle walked out through her great room sliding doors, into the courtyard garden. Already it was starting to look lovely. Jodie had planted a lot of flowers as an underlayer to the shrubs, and the first of them were already in bloom, making a pretty picture of color against the green shrubs. Tenealle drew a deep breath into her lungs. There was a special scent to the garden too. Not a definable one, just an earthy, growing sort of smell. It made the air seem fresher, cleaner somehow, despite being in the city.

She sat on the side of the fountain and trailed one hand in the water. It was cool and clear, and the fountain made a bubbling noise that provided a happy background to the garden.

Tenealle pulled her hand out of the water and patted the stonework. "You're happier now you're all cleaned up, aren't you?" she asked rhetorically.

"Oh, yes, and I do like seeing flowers in my garden again, too. When are you going to buy my fish?"

Tenealle jumped up and turned around quickly, her hands against her pounding heart. "All right, which of you cousins nearly scared me to death?" she asked, her voice still quavering a bit. "And how did you get in? The door's locked."

"Oh no, dear, I'm not one of your cousins. Although you do have such a lot of them. My name is Mary, and I'm so glad you moved in here. I miss Enid. We knew each other for nearly fifty years."

Tenealle looked all around the garden again and walked to the great room doorway, but no one was teasing her. Only when she shook her head in disbelief did she see the shimmery, wavering figure standing inside the fountain. She shook her head again, harder, and blinked her eyes. The figure was still there, and the woman was smiling at her.

"Mary?"

"That's right, dear. This is my fountain and my garden. I live here."

"You live here?"

"This warehouse building was originally my home, and this was the rooftop garden. This is the only piece that has remained unchanged. Enid and I spent a lot of time sitting out here in the sunshine and chatting. I've really missed her," Mary finished simply.

"I'm—I'm pleased to meet you, Mary. I hope you'll be happy here once again," said Tenealle, gathering the shreds of the manners her mama had taught her as child, even though her mind was screaming, *Ghost? Mirage? Have I been breathing in too many cleaning products?*

"It's been lovely hearing young voices and seeing young people around the garden again. But I do miss the fish. You were serious about replacing them, weren't you?"

"Yes, yes, I am. It sounded like an awesome idea. I'll do that at the weekend. How do you feel about a small dog living here, too?" Tenealle asked a little hesitantly, wondering if talking to a ghost was a sign of incipient insanity.

"Ah, my dear little Sultan passed on a long time before I did, and I never had the heart to replace him. But a doggie would be good company for both of us, I believe."

"Sultan. That's a good name for a dog. It'll be a few more weeks yet before I can organize time to go to the animal shelter for a dog, but the fish will be no problem. They're easy to care for."

"That would be lovely, dear. Your young men are here. Enid was so proud of Evan. He's a fine man, a credit to his family." Mary seemed to disappear into the stone of the fountain.

Tenealle stood there for a moment, still wondering if she was hallucinating from cleaning product fumes, when the doorbell rang. Shaking her head yet again, she went to collect her purse and go out with Evan and Faris.

* * * *

The bathroom exhibition was a lot of fun, and Tenealle collected an enormous pile of glossy brochures. Even the men were interested in the displays, so the three found a lot to discuss. Finally they had gone full circle around the building and were back at the entrance. Only then did Tenealle realize how much her feet ached and how late it was getting.

Evan wrapped his arm around her and asked, "Had enough? You look exhausted."

"Yes, let's go home."

"Our place, I think. I don't want you trying to measure up things or search for electrical outlets or anything more tonight. By the way, why do you always look for electrical outlets everywhere we go?" asked Faris.

"Because I prefer to vacuum rather than sweep," she answered absent-mindedly trying to remember how many flights of stairs she needed to walk down before they reached the parking lot.

"Huh?" "Say what?" the men responded together, sharing confused looks over the top of her head.

"When you sweep, the dust gets spread around even farther. When you vacuum, the dust is sucked up inside the bag, and it's done," she explained.

"Tenealle, we're guys. We do know what a vacuum cleaner is, but can you explain the relationship between looking at electrical outlets everywhere you go, and a vacuum cleaner, a little more lucidly please?"

"Yeah, maybe use words of one syllable so a mere man can understand," added Evan.

She laughed, then explained. "Because I work from home, I often use my break time to do a household chore. But because I'm on a strict time limit—if I don't work, I don't get paid—I only do one thing at a time. So I would never vacuum more than one room at a time. This means I plug the vacuum in a particular room and vacuum it, then go back to the day job. If there is no electrical outlet, I have to get out an extension cord, get it all set up, then vacuum, and then put it all away. It's just too much hassle. So I need a vacuum-cleaner-accessible electrical outlet in every room.

"Ahh, now it makes sense," said Faris, unlocking the car and ushering Tenealle inside.

"You know, woman, you're crazy. But it's a good kind of crazy," said Evan, lifting her feet onto his lap and massaging her arches.

Tenealle sighed in bliss as his clever fingers soothed all the tension and untangled knots she didn't even know she'd had in her foot muscles. By the time they arrived at the men's apartment, she was relaxed, yet aroused, happy and contented, yet more than ready for sex.

They undressed quietly, then snuggled together on the bed. As happened frequently, the men put her between them, one pressed to her front, the other plastered along her back, and their arms wrapped around each other so she was firmly held in the middle.

But tonight Tenealle wanted to do things differently.

"That foot massage was excellent. I want to play with you both." She wiggled, and they loosened their arms, letting her sit up. "Hmm. I think you should lie on your backs first."

Obligingly they rolled onto their backs.

Tenealle thought for a moment. She didn't want to copy Evan by massaging their feet. And she didn't really want to repeat the time she'd tied them up with their own neckties, assuming they'd even let her try such a game again. So what could she do?

She leaned forward to let her hair trail over their torsos, flipping it this way and that lightly, teasingly, angling her head so it trailed over their chests and their abs.

She held a handful of hair in one hand and teased it around their nipples, swirled it around their belly buttons, and drew it down toward their cocks. Cocks that were growing longer as she watched them. Bellies that were developing goose bumps.

Faris's breath hitched as she turned to him and scraped her fingernail across one of his nipples. Both men's gazes were focused on her, their eyes swiveling with every movement she made. That gave her an idea.

Tenealle bent toward Evan, her hand out as if to touch him on the face or neck. His head dipped a little so he could watch her. Like a magician's sleight-of-hand trick, while both men were concentrated on her hand near Evan's face, she used the fingers of her other hand to tease his thigh. His chest rose and fell faster, and she knew she'd successfully aroused both men a little more with that tactic.

Extrapolating from there, she nudged their legs with her knees and wiggled her butt across their legs, back and forth, bending her body and swaying. As she'd hoped, their eyes followed her movements.

This time she grasped both cocks in one hand and rubbed them together against each other.

"Holy shit," groaned Faris.

Evan just gasped.

Tenealle settled herself properly over their legs and began stroking their cocks smoothly from root to cap, root to cap, using both hands now. Then she pressed her fingers along the big veins as she twisted the cocks before tracing the shafts with her nails.

Finally she leaned down and licked first one head, then the other, running her tongue into each slit to catch the drops of pre-cum beading there.

"Enough," said Evan hoarsely. "Daisy chain."

They formed a loose triangle, Evan's head at her pussy, hers at Faris's cock, and Faris's mouth on Evan's cock.

Tenealle concentrated on sucking deeply, relaxing the back of her throat to take as much as possible of Faris, then letting him slide almost out as she nibbled along his stalk and around his cock head. She knew how sensitive the ridge joining head and shaft was, and tried hard to press with her tongue at just the right place to arouse him intensely.

But it was so hard for her to concentrate with the delicious things Evan was doing to her pussy. His licking, sucking, and nibbling on her folds and her clit were driving her to an orgasm so fast she despaired of having time to properly pleasure Faris.

Someone's hand reached out to tweak her nipple, and someone was stroking her leg. Tenealle couldn't think, couldn't concentrate, and could scarcely remember to breathe.

Frantically she sucked Faris deep down her throat, hollowing her cheeks for extra pressure. Then she hummed, hoping the vibrations would give him as much pleasure as she was receiving.

It must have worked because a thick stream of cum erupted into her mouth just as Evan bit her clit.

Her mouth opened automatically to scream in pleasure, and she had to consciously make herself close it to suck Faris as he spurted again. Evan's rhythmic shaking reassured her that he, too, had climaxed, and she relaxed into her orgasm, letting the waves wash across her and carry her with them, her mind free and her body shaking in delight.

Then arms and legs were tangling with hers as she was hauled up the bed so all three heads were sharing the one pillow and she was tucked securely between her men.

"Good teamwork," she mumbled, feeling herself drift into sleep in their arms.

Chapter Five

Tenealle stood up from her computer and stretched, easing the kinks out of her back, rolling her shoulders, shaking her ankles. She couldn't help but notice no cousins had descended on her since the day she'd moved in, and while her bad angel was singing and dancing in joy about this, her good angel was nagging her that maybe Evan and Faris had something to do with her vanishing cousins. And that maybe she should say something about it.

She kneeled on the office floor with a tape measure, pencil, and piece of paper, writing measurements, drawing a floor plan, and calculating how many tiles she'd need to buy, but all the time her bad angel and good angel were arguing in her head.

By the time she'd finished the math, she'd decided. *I'll talk to Evan and Faris about it tonight.*

But it seemed they'd come to some sort of decision, too, as Faris rang only half an hour later.

"Um, honey, would it be okay if we go to your cousin Herb's tonight for a bit of a chat?"

"You only ever call me honey when you're suggesting something you think I might not like. Define 'chat.'"

"Well, um, it's about your shoes."

"My shoes? I thought we'd gotten past that. It was just a stupid prank."

"Well, um—"

There were some strange noises on the line before Evan spoke. "God, Faris, sometimes you're useless. Tenealle, we know who put that stuff in your shoes and why. But we want them to tell you themselves. So how about we pick you up at seven and go to Herb and Delores's place?"

"Have you two been keeping my cousins away from me?"

"Not exactly."

"Define—"

"We'll tell you everything tonight. We'll pick you up at seven." Evan hung up.

Tenealle stood looking at her cell for a while, then shrugged. *I was going to talk to them tonight anyway, so nothing's changed really.*

* * * *

The men had obviously planned their strategy carefully, because they kept up an unbroken stream of inconsequential chitchat from the moment she opened her front door to them, until Herb opened his to the three of them.

She shot Evan and Faris a fierce look. "Don't think you fooled me for a minute with that tactic. We'll discuss it later," she said.

She could almost feel their grins on her back as they followed her inside.

In Herbert's great room stood Delores, Emma and Steve, and Nick and Nate. Mentally, Tenealle patted herself on the back. She'd thought Nate and Nick were the most likely culprits, and here they were. Well, she was interested to hear what they thought they were achieving by the prank.

But it was Steve who was shuffling from foot to foot and refusing to look her in the eye, and Emma looked mighty unhappy with him.

"I bought it on the Internet. Cost me fifty dead presidents, plus shipping. And it wasn't even magic witch's powder. It was drain cleaner. Drain cleaner! Two bucks in Wal-Mart," he said aggrievedly.

Tenealle kept a tight grip on her urge to laugh and asked gently, "But why did you buy it, Steve? I don't understand."

"It was supposed to make you go away. They said it was a disappear spell. I thought Mr. and Mrs. Jones would like me better if you weren't around. They're always talking about you. In fact, the whole fucking family is always talking about you. Everyone likes you." The aggrieved tone was still strong in his voice.

"And now even Emma doesn't like me anymore." His tone had become plaintive. It appeared he genuinely liked Emma.

Steve stood taller, aged several years before Tenealle's eyes. "I'd like to apologize, Ms. Jones. It was a dead stupid thing to do, and I'm sorry. I had no wish to hurt you or anything. I just wanted you to go away."

He looked her in the eye, and she knew he was speaking the truth.

"That's fine, Steve. I forgive you. I wasn't hurt, thanks to Mark throwing me in the pool. Fortunately, Evan was quick enough to rinse his hands, so he wasn't hurt either. Likely, you have learned a few important lessons from this experience."

Steve grinned. "Yeah, don't buy nothing off the Internet, and don't believe witches." He turned to Herbert and Delores. "I apologize for my behavior. It was stupid and childish. Good-bye." Then he turned to Emma. His face seemed to crumple a little before he straightened his shoulders and said, "I'm very sorry, Emma. I never wanted to upset you."

Nodding at the others in the great room, Steve turned and left. There was just the faint sound of his shoes on the tiles, then a quiet snick as the front door closed behind him.

Tenealle sent a questioning look at Nick and Nate.

"We knew he had something planned."

"But we didn't know what it was."

"We never would have wanted you to be hurt."

"We're really sorry, Cuz."

"Yeah."

"That's okay, I understand," Tenealle replied.

Nick and Nate nodded to Herb and left.

"So that's it. No plot, no bad motive or evil intent, just a young man trying to impress his girlfriend's family?"

"That's about it," said Herb.

Emma threw herself into Tenealle's arms. "I'm sorry, Tenealle. How could I have thought I liked such a dickhead?"

"He wasn't so bad. But it seems he did need to do some growing up." Tenealle hugged her back.

"Yeah, I reckon the Terrible Twosome have done some growing up in a hurry too," added Delores. "Now, let's eat. I made coleslaw, potato salad, and chicken-fried steaks."

* * * *

The Domain was full of cousins. Cousins sitting on the floor, talking. Cousins leaning against the wall, talking, all with pizza in one hand, paper cup of soda in the other. Out in the courtyard, a few young third or fourth cousins were running around with Sultan the puppy, kicking a soccer ball, and laughing and screaming in joy.

Sitting on the side of the fountain was Katie. She was maybe five or six years old, a cute, pigtailed blonde, and she seemed to be chatting away to herself. Or maybe to the goldfish who now lived in the fountain.

Tenealle stepped out into the courtyard with a tray of pizza and sodas to see if any of the children were still hungry or thirsty. She looked at Katie, her gaze following the direction of Katie's gaze. Very faint in the bright sunshine was the shimmery outline of a woman in the fountain. Mary! Katie was talking to Mary.

Tenealle walked through the garden to the fountain. Katie jumped up, grabbed a soda, and ran across to Sultan.

Mary smiled at her and nodded. "Katie sees me too, Tenealle, just as you do. You and Evan and Faris will be happy here for many years. Like Enid was with her Arthur. And just as she knew the right person to leave this garden to was Evan, when the time comes, you will know what to do."

"I guess Katie may be the one, huh?" said Tenealle.

"You won't need to make any decisions for a very long time. You will have a wonderful future with those men."

"As crazy as it sounds, Steve did me a favor putting that drain cleaner in my shoes. It made me realize what Evan and Faris and I had was more than just an affair, more than just sex. Their fiercely protective response showed me they genuinely cared for me."

"I knew they would move in here with you. Evan simply needed to see how you spruced the place up again first."

"I think he needed the space between his aunt and me. It was too much for him to face at the start. But it brought us together, so him selling it was obviously the right thing to do," Tenealle replied.

"Thank you for the goldfish. And thank you, too, for Sultan II. I love seeing him out here, playing with the children."

"The fish and the puppy were wonderful ideas. Besides, having you here makes the Domain even more special for me," Tenealle replied, mere moments before she was bombarded by a group of children all demanding pizza.

* * * *

Gradually the cousins started to leave, all of them still chattering about how good the apartment looked now, and all of them promising to come for a visit again soon.

Tenealle groaned, but Faris and Evan laughed. "Lucky we decided to keep our apartment as a cousins' guesthouse when we moved in here with you," joked Faris.

"And so far, you don't use nearly as much hot water as Tim, or eat as much as Mark, so it's all good," she replied.

Jack and Drew came up to say good-bye. "I'll be back for another Scrabble competition next month. There will be food in the refrigerator at your place, won't there?" he asked Faris, hopefully.

Tenealle laughed. "Of course. And we'll come and watch you play, too."

They closed the door behind the last few cousins to leave, then walked back down the hallway to the kitchen. Tenealle was thrilled to see it was sparkling clean, the trash all neatly stacked in bags, and a note on the refrigerator door saying, *This is your housewarming present, Mark and Jodie.*

"Wow! Now that's a neat present!" said Tenealle.

"Ow! Bad pun," replied Evan, making them all laugh.

"I believe your cousins are growing on me. I actually like them all. But I'm glad they've finally gone and we can just be us, together, a family," said Faris, wrapping his arms around both Evan and Tenealle and pulling them tight against his chest for a bear hug.

Sultan ran inside and barked at their feet, begging to be picked up.

"Yeah, you too, furball." Faris grinned.

"He should be exhausted after playing with the kids for hours," Evan added, giving Sultan a hug, then settling him in his bed in a corner of the room.

Tenealle refilled his water dish but left the food bowl empty. "I suspect the kids gave you more than enough pizza, and you won't need any doggie treats tonight." She mock-frowned at him.

Evan came up behind her and pressed against her back. His cock was a hard ridge in the crack of her ass. "What about me? Are there any treats for me?"

"Oh, I think I might be able to find one or two." She smiled back over her shoulder at him.

"Sounds yummy." Faris was enveloping her from the front. His cock pressed into her belly, his arms around her shoulders and drawing Evan closer to them both.

Tenealle loved being like this. She was totally encompassed by hard, hot males who genuinely cared for her and enjoyed her as a person as well as a woman. Sure, she loved her cousins, who were interesting people and mostly good fun to be around, but her feelings for these two men were so much deeper. Like the difference between the water in the fountain and the depths of the ocean. Evan and Faris had opened for her a door into a whole new world of emotions. And she felt as though she had just begun to explore the height and depth of the passion between them. It was still growing and growing inside her every minute she spent with them, whether they were with other people or alone, in bed or in public.

She wanted to bury herself in them, learn all about them, share herself with them. But right now, some scorching-hot sex sounded very good to her. Just seeing them, being with them, having them wrap their arms around her made her panties damp and her pussy ache and yearn to be filled by one or the other of them. Her ass clenched too. Having one of them there would be good too. Or in her mouth. Anywhere.

Faris swept her off her feet and walked through the great room and out into the courtyard.

"What? I thought we were about to have sex?"

"Oh, we are, we are."

"I hate to break it to you, but the bedroom is in the opposite direction," she pointed out.

"Yeah. But we've made love in the bed lots of times. We've never made love on the fountain before."

"On the fountain?" Tenealle hoped she hadn't screeched those words, but she rather thought she might have. *Sex? On the fountain?*

"Yep, the ledge is very wide," Evan added helpfully.

"Well, it's a hot enough day. I don't suppose it'll matter if we fall in," she agreed, although her brain was still coming to grips with the concept. She hoped they'd thought about how this would work because it wasn't obvious to her.

"It might startle the fish, I suppose, but we'll be naked anyway," added Faris, putting her down and pulling her T-shirt over her head all in the same, single, fluid motion.

She kicked her sandals off as the men toed off their shoes. Then four hands were tugging at her skirt, and it puddled around her feet very quickly.

She grabbed the nearest T-shirt and peeled it up a ripped torso— Evan's—before lowering her hand to his zipper. For a few minutes, six hands were everywhere on the three bodies, removing the last of their clothing, before Faris pulled a tube of lube and a string of condoms from one of the pockets in his cargo pants.

"See, those years I spent in the Boy Scouts weren't wasted!" he joked.

"Good to know," Tenealle replied, her breath catching in her throat as she assimilated the delicious picture the men presented. Their bodies were lit by the sunlight, dappled a little by the shade of a live oak. Faris's hair shone golden in the afternoon light, and Evan's was such a beautiful, rich, dark brown it reminded her of the most expensive—and delicious—chocolate. *Damn, they're hot. And they're mine!*

Faris sat on the side of the fountain, his legs spread wide, his cock standing straight up, ready for action. He rolled a condom down his shaft, then nodded to Evan.

"Come closer, and let Tenealle and me get you ready for this party."

"Hell yeah. I do like being the ham in the sandwich."

Evan straddled Faris's thighs, facing away from him, bent forward so his butt was at the right height for Faris to lube his dark channel.

He drew Tenealle closer to him and rested his face on her breasts, holding her around the waist. "You're so beautiful, our every dream come true. I love your breasts, always so soft and ripe. Your nipples are like berries just waiting for us to suck them into our mouths." Evan suited the actions to the words, sucking a nipple deep into the hot cavern of his mouth, rolling his tongue around the nipple, teasing the areola, then using his tongue to press her nipple to the roof of his mouth.

Desire roared through Tenealle, from her nipples directly to her pussy, her belly clenching with need. She pressed her breasts into his face, grabbing hold of his shoulders to steady herself, as her legs were suddenly weak with the force of her pleasure.

As she pressed into him, she could feel Faris's fingers in Evan's ass, feel the swirling movements he was making, feel Evan's cock pressed into her belly, twitching with his own need to come, and the dampness at his cock head that indicated just how very ready he was.

"Enough. I can't wait. Any more of this double stimulation and the party will be over before it's begun," gasped Evan hoarsely after letting Tenealle's nipple pop out of his mouth.

Faris dropped the lube onto the flagstones and pulled on Evan's hips to turn him around. Tenealle watched closely as Evan sank down onto Faris's cock. Observing that engorged shaft gradually slide into the welcoming channel was the hottest thing Tenealle had ever seen! She was so wet and ready for this. Her empty cunt was aching to be filled, her breasts in agony from Evan's touch. All she wanted, needed, was a cock inside her right now.

When Faris had sunk inside Evan to the absolute hilt, Evan rolled a condom onto his cock. Tenealle stood on the fountain, then carefully stepped one leg over Evan and let him guide his cock into her pussy as she gradually squatted down, her back to Evan, her face to Faris. Finally she was sitting on Evan's lap, with Evan on top of Faris.

She clung tightly to Faris's neck. He had his arms around Evan's hips, enclosing her between them, and Evan placed his arms around Faris, doubling their hold on her.

Jerkily at first, then moving more smoothly and in time with each other, Faris thrust up into Evan, and Evan into Tenealle. She just held on for the ride. Every pulse from both cocks was transferred into her body by their actions. Every movement, every twist was amplified through Evan, and into her. It was so intense, so powerful, so amazing, Tenealle could hardly get her mind around what they were doing. All she knew was that the biggest orgasm of her life was building and building inside her.

Using their feet—Faris's on the flagstones, Evan's on the fountain—and their thigh muscles, the men kept thrusting up, faster, harder, deeper. Soon they were absolutely pistoning into each other, and Tenealle dug her nails into Faris's shoulders as the first ripples of her climax rolled through her pussy. Her orgasm exploded through her, crashing through every nerve ending, blasting out her arms and legs, curling her toes, almost blowing the top off her head.

She couldn't hold back the scream that tore from her throat as her orgasm went on and on. Evan's cock sent streams of hot cum burning through the latex in her pussy, the pulses simply intensifying her orgasm. Even as she cried out in release, she could feel Faris's cock exploding in Evan's ass. Their three bodies were so linked together, their sensations so attuned to each other.

The men thrust in and out a few more times, their cocks still pulsing with release, as the ripples in Tenealle's belly gradually quieted down and her muscles unlocked. Finally the three sank into each other's arms, their bodies coated with sweat, their muscles now loose and relaxed.

"Best. Orgasm. Ever," whispered Tenealle.

"Absolutely."

"Hell yeah. And we didn't even fall into the fountain," added Faris.

"Haven't fallen in yet. We still have to untangle ourselves, but I don't think I will be able to stand up for a while," said Tenealle.

"No rush," said Evan, snuggling into the other two, his arms still wrapped around them both. "I love the time we spend together like this. I love you both so much."

"I love you both, too." Tenealle twisted her neck to kiss first Evan, then Faris.

"Love you," Faris murmured into her hair as he lightly punched Evan's upper arm.

Tenealle lifted her head from Faris's shoulder and looked at the fountain. For a moment she thought her vision was still blurry from the force of her orgasm. But then she realized the faint figure of Mary was almost within touching distance. Tenealle's mouth sagged open, and her jaw dropped.

Mary just smiled and winked at Tenealle.

I guess that means she's given us her blessing. Tenealle looked straight at the ghost and mouthed the words *Thank you.*

Mary nodded and disappeared.

THE END

http://berengariabrown.webs.com/

ABOUT THE AUTHOR

Berengaria is a multi-published author of erotic romance: contemporary, paranormal (ghosts, vampires and werewolves) and Regency-set historical. She loves to read all different kinds of romance so that is what she writes: one man/one woman; two women; two men; two men/one woman; three men….Whatever the characters need for their very hot happily-ever-after, Berengaria makes sure they get it.

Also by Berengaria Brown

Ménage Amour: Forever Yours 1: *Intensity*
Ménage Amour: Forever Yours 2: *Complexity*
Ménage Amour: Forever Yours 3: *Eternity*
Ménage Amour: Possessive Passions 1: *Shared Possession*
Ménage Amour: Possessive Passions 2: *Possess Me*
Ménage Amour: Possessive Passions 3: *Ultimate Possession*

Available at
BOOKSTRAND.COM

Siren Publishing, Inc.
www.SirenPublishing.com